'I don't believe fanciful ideas.

'Not even the one about avoiding the sight of a man with a harelip—or a disfiguring scar?' Richard's voice had become cold and clipped. 'I thought you were frightened to death about that.'

Pamela was appalled. 'You are mistaken,' she stammered, 'I wasn't aware—I didn't want you to think—'

He put a hand over hers. 'My dear child, I've known ever since our wedding day that you can hardly bear to look at me. If I hadn't been so slow-witted I'd have guessed at once, before we became engaged. I thought you were simply nervous and shy. And then we were married so soon, on account of your father's health. If I'd guessed the truth I'd never have gone through with it.'

Sheila Bishop was born in London and spent a wandering childhood while her father was in the regular army. She lived in South America for several years and had twice been through the Magellan Straits before she was nine. Later she returned to England, living first in the country and later in London and Essex. She worked as a shorthand typist with the Foreign Office and during the war did secretarial and welfare work with the British Red Cross Society, spending some time in North Africa and Italy—where she met her husband. She now lives in Bath, Somerset, and has one daughter. She has written many Regency and Elizabethan romances, and this is her third Masquerade Historical Romance.

A MARRIAGE
MADE ON EARTH

Sheila Bishop

First published in Great Britain 1990
by Mills & Boon Limited

© Sheila Bishop 1990

Australian copyright 1990
Philippine copyright 1990
This edition 1990

ISBN 0 263 77081 8

Masquerade is a trademark published by
Mills & Boon Limited, Eton House,
18–24 Paradise Road, Richmond, Surrey, TW9 1SR.

Set in Times Roman 10½ on 12 pt.
04-9012-68251 C

Made and printed in Great Britain

CHAPTER ONE

BECAUSE she was so preoccupied with her own feelings of resentment and despair, Pamela Stonebridge did not hear the sound of horses approaching round the blind corner beyond the parsonage. She was standing in the middle of the quiet country lane when she was suddenly overtaken by a curricle and pair which appeared out of nowhere and nearly knocked her into the ditch.

She jumped back and got a flying impression of a pair of black horses, wheels, and a man with a driving-whip perched high above them. The man turned his head and shouted at her. He had a dark, lined face and an ugly, jeering expression.

Mannerless brute, she thought. He was driving much too fast and had no business to swear at her. She was sure he had been swearing.

Strangely enough, the curricle had slowed down. Was he going to come back and apologise? She hoped not, for she had not liked his looks. She stood still, watching, and then realised what was happening. The stranger had reined in his horses just outside the entrance to her own home, waiting for the lodge-keeper to throw open the gates. A few seconds later he was driving up the avenue towards Crewse Manor.

The truth came home to her with a shock of incredulity. That was her unknown bridegroom, the hateful person her parents had chosen for her in such a high-handed fashion.

'I won't marry him,' she said aloud. 'I won't do it.'

She slipped back into the grounds of the manor by way of a copse which bordered the road, and began to walk up and down between the trees, reliving that very disagreeable conversation with her parents when they had told her she was going to marry Lord Blaise. She had protested indignantly.

'I don't want to marry Lord Blaise. He is a horrid old man and he has mistresses.'

Not *that* Lord Blaise, they had assured her hastily. He died last year. This was his son.

'Well, I don't want to marry him either. He drinks like a fish.'

She had picked up this information some time ago when she had been visiting her godmother Lady Emden at Ramsgate. Other guests in the house had gossiped about the dissolute habits of the Cressinder family, who were related to Lady Emden. That was all she had even heard about them, for they lived in quite another county, south-west of London.

Her mother had begun to explain.

'I'm afraid the elder son was very unsteady, poor fellow. He died a few weeks before his father. The present baron is his younger brother Richard, a former cavalry officer who served in Spain and afterwards at Waterloo. He is a man of exemplary character.'

Pamela had not believed her, and the creature in the curricle had proved to be exactly what one might have expected.

The most bewildering thing about the whole business had been the behaviour of her parents, who had suddenly announced that they had chosen a husband for her and that he was arriving today to pay his addresses. What could have induced them to take up such a Gothic attitude? They had always loved her and, until now, had never tried to coerce her, but, today, when she had begun to argue with her father, he had become extremely angry, calling her ungrateful and disobedient and threatening to lock her up until she came to her senses. Then he had started a violent fit of coughing which was likely to bring on one of his spasms, so that her mama too had turned against her, calling her selfish and thoughtless.

As though I ought to let my life be ruined rather than upset Papa, thought Pamela, aggrieved. She felt guilty all the same, for her father's health was precarious and he could not bear any great strain on his heart. Her parents were so old, she supposed that was the real trouble; they might have been her grandparents. Their own very happy marriage had been arranged for them by their families, which had been quite the accepted practice when they were young though it seemed positively archaic today.

Pamela was seventeen, the same age as the century, and most of her life had been lived during the long war against Bonaparte. Extraordinary to realise that Papa and Mama had been married before the French Revolution.

She gazed about her in the wood, hardly taking in the signs of spring, the interlacing branches of the trees whose thin young leaves were just uncurling in the fresh green of April.

She was a tall, thin girl, a little too thin. Her hair, which had been red when she was a child, was now much fairer, the colour of pale, new-minted copper. Fashionably cropped and smooth, it was inclined to break loose and bubble in curls all over her head. She had clear grey eyes and a dazzling skin. Her features were too irregular to be called beautiful, though Ben Watney had said she was like a missing figure from the Botticelli 'Primavera'.

It was to Ben that she had run instinctively for comfort as soon as she could escape from the house. He was the third son of the rector and the love of her life. Full of her own disastrous news, she had not remembered until she was nearly at the parsonage that Ben would not be there today. He had planned to go fishing. That was why she had been standing stupidly in the middle of the road, wondering what to do next, when the villainous Lord Blaise had come round the corner and nearly run her down.

And perhaps it was as well, she thought, that I wasn't able to see Ben, for, after all, what could he do? Although she was impulsive she was not silly, and she knew that an Oxford undergraduate of nineteen could not come forward and offer to marry her himself. Ben was an extremely handsome and clever young man who intended to enter the Church. He could not be ordained until he was twenty-four, and after that he might still have to wait several years before he could obtain the sort of preferment which would enable him to marry. She was sure her father would not allow her to embark on such a long, uncertain engagement, even if he had not already struck some kind of bargain with that horrid lord. She did wonder for a moment whether she could persuade Ben to run off to Scotland with her, but she knew he would never agree. He was far too good and honourable. He had never even made her an open declaration because he said he had no right to.

Pamela gave a deep sigh. It was not that she really wanted to go to Scotland—elopements were dreadfully vulgar—she simply wanted to escape the prospect that faced her at home. She was gripped by a sense of growing panic. The idea of marrying that man with the jeering mouth disgusted her. She had seen him only for a brief moment but was convinced that he had all the vices of his dissolute father and brother. Surely Mama would realise that, even if Papa was blinded by the wretched man's title and consequence. If only she could run away by herself so that she would not have to meet him, but where could she go?

She had plenty of friends who would sympathise with her plight and some of them had parents who would also sympathise, but none of them, she was afraid, would be prepared to conceal her from her own parents.

Then it struck her that she need not actually run anywhere. All she had to do was to disappear for long enough to convince everyone that she had run away sooner than marry her unwelcome suitor. He would then be obliged to retire, and, no matter how angry her father was, the marriage plan would be at an end.

So where was she to hide? She was turning over possibilities in her mind as she made her way home, and, after rejecting all the outbuildings for various reasons, she formed a daring scheme. She would hide in the house itself.

The present manor house at Crewse had been built in the last century on the site of a much inferior dwelling which the Stonebridge family had put up with for hundreds of years. It stood proudly in its pretty park, an urbane square of red brick, like a house in a sampler, she had sometimes thought. She made a cautious circuit and went in by the back door.

She lurked in the recesses of a cold, clean passage, knowing that sooner or later an ally would appear. Not one of the upper servants who would feel obliged to side with her parents, but someone nearer her own age. She was on good terms with them all.

Presently she caught sight of a small, thin girl, smothered in a cap and apron that were much too large for her.

'Biddy—come here!' whispered Pamela urgently.

'Mercy, Miss Pam—you did give me a start!'

'Keep your voice down. I want you to do something for me. I'm going up to the attic and I don't want anyone to know I'm in the house. I want you to get me some food out of the pantry. Bread, apples, it doesn't matter what. Anything that won't be missed. And you must pretend you haven't seen me, not that anyone is likely to ask. Do you understand?'

'No, Miss Pam,' said Biddy truthfully.

'Well, never mind. There's someone in the house I don't want to meet, that's all.'

'Would it be the lord?' enquired Biddy.

The question sounded so biblical that Pamela had a wild desire to giggle. Without answering directly, she said, 'You will help me, won't you?'

'Oh, yes, Miss Pam. Thomas said he never saw a gentleman look so terrible.'

So I didn't imagine that dreadful expression, thought Pamela with a shudder. She waited for Biddy to fetch her provisions. The girl soon came back with a basket containing a hunk of cheese, a small raised pie and several apples.

Pamela went quietly up the back stairs to the top of the house, meeting no one. This was the servants' staircase, not much in use in the afternoon. The maids all slept on the top floor. There were several rooms unoccupied, one of them full of discarded furniture, and in here she made a nest for herself, sitting on a pile of faded curtains and leaning against a broken settee.

She wondered very much what was happening downstairs and how her parents were dealing with that monster, which was how she had begun to think of Lord Blaise. They had not been able to produce an amenable bride for his inspection, so he was probably making himself very disagreeable by now. She hoped he was. That might cause even Papa to think again.

She guessed they would also be trying to find out where she had gone—surreptitiously, while keeping up a calm façade and making lame excuses for her absence.

She was sitting beside one of the little round windows which ran along the whole length of the house under the balustrade. Presently she saw their own barouche going sedately down the drive with the old coachman on the box. Where could he be going at this hour? The answer was plain. Her parents had sent him out, with many tactful messages no doubt, to make a round of their neighbours' houses in search of their absconding daughter.

Pamela began to feel guilty. It was wrong to frighten them so. Then she realised that if they had been genuinely frightened there would have been searchers out on foot in case she had met with an accident. Sending the barouche was a proof that they knew she was hiding from the monster.

The stable clock chimed five. This was dinnertime at the manor and Pamela decided to eat her provisions. She felt hollow rather than hungry. The pie and the cheese gave her a burning thirst which the apples could not quench and the idea of spending the night up here with nothing to drink soon became intolerable. Suppose she were to creep down to the floor below and fetch some water and a few other luxuries? A candle and a book perhaps, and a shawl, for, although the curtains would keep her warm, they were very dusty.

This was the one time in the evening when there would be very little risk of being caught, for her parents and their guest would be anchored in the dining-room for well over an hour and the maids too would still be down on the ground floor. She got up, glad to move, for she was getting stiff, and started down the uncarpeted back stairs. When she reached the first floor she waited, listening, before she opened the door on to the central landing. Not a sound. She slipped through, closing the door again with great care.

The high, rectangular landing was lit from a sky-light overhead and there was nothing whatever to be seen except the bland white surfaces of a great many other closed doors. All were exactly alike: the entrances to the back stairs, the front stairs and several bedrooms. There were even two sham doors that didn't open at all and had been put there by the architect to create a perfect symmetry.

Pamela's own bedroom was next to the front staircase. Once inside she felt safe. She helped herself to a long drink from the water jug, noting the can of hot water which had been placed in her wash-basin by the maid who had laid out on the bed the prettiest of her white gauze dresses to wear at dinner. She wondered about the trio in the dining-room and how they were getting on without her.

In fact she had miscalculated. Dinner had been put back an hour. Five was unfashionably early and her mother had decided all along that they could not expect Lord Blaise to dine before six.

'And a good thing too,' Mrs Stonebridge was saying to her maid as she adjusted a smart lace cap before the looking-glass in her bedroom. 'We can delay dinner for a further half-hour if Miss Pamela isn't home by then. I wish I knew which of her friends she went to call on. So thoughtless of her to be late, today of all days...'

The maid murmured something consoling. Neither woman was deceived. One knew and the other guessed why Pamela had not come home and Mrs Stonebridge was nearing her wits' end over what to do next. The elderly mother of such a young daughter, she now looked tired and wan. She had never taken to modern fashions and still wore the high-piled hair and full skirts of her youth. The eyes that met her on the surface of the looking-glass looked permanently anxious.

Only a few yards away across the landing, Pamela had decided to make use of the hot water. She would wash and change into a warmer, more comfortable dress before spending the night in the attic. She had taken off her creased morning gown and was standing in her petticoat when her door opened and she heard a strange masculine voice exclaim, 'Good God—I beg your pardon! I mistook the door.'

Pamela did not see him but she knew who he must be. She made a dive for the concealing chintz curtains that hung round her bed. Then she heard her mother on the landing.

'Are you looking for the staircase, Lord Blaise? These doors are so confusing. That is my daughter's room.'

'Yes, I know, ma'am. I'm so sorry. I hope Miss Stonebridge was not too much alarmed.'

'Do you mean to say she's in there?' Quite forgetting to play the gracious hostess, Mrs Stonebridge almost ran into the room. 'Pamela, where have you been?'

'I went for a walk, Mama,' said Pamela, still clinging to the bed curtain.

Mrs Stonebridge closed the door. 'You must get dressed at once and come down to dinner.'

'I don't want to come down. I don't want to meet that man.'

Her mother drew a deep breath, as though she was trying to hold on to the last shreds of self-command.

'I know you don't at present wish to marry Lord Blaise and you think Papa and I have been unkind in making this match without consulting you. I think myself we should have been more open with you and I promise I will explain the situation to you later, but in the meantime you must come down to dinner. You may refuse an offer of marriage; you cannot refuse to meet a guest in your father's house. Such a discourtesy would put us all to shame. So put on your dress and don't argue.'

'Yes, Mama,' said Pamela, daunted by something in her mother's manner which she had never met before.

A few minutes later she found herself, virginal and shivering slightly in the white gauze, entering the drawing-room. Her first proper view of Lord Blaise was in profile as he sat sideways on to the door and she had a sudden surprise, for there was no sign of the haggard, leering monster, simply a youngish man with strong features, not handsome but not at all disagreeable. Then he stood up and turned towards her and she saw the other side of his face and what it was she had taken for an expression of satanic depravity. There was a deep, unsightly scar running from the temple down past the cheekbone to the corner of his mouth. It creased the flesh and pulled the corner of his eye and his upper lip a little out of alignment. She found the result quite shocking.

When he was introduced to her, she was unable to speak, which did not matter, because he probably thought that this was due to shyness, and her father was breaking in, demanding to know where she had been, sounding more concerned than angry. He said he had been worried to death, and then tried to laugh it off, because Pamela's eligible suitor must not be given the idea that anything was wrong.

'Young women have no notion of time! You'll find that out, my dear Blaise, if you don't know it already.'

They went in to dinner. It was a painful meal. Pamela could not eat—she had already gobbled up the meat pie and all the cheese. She sat opposite Blaise, managing not to look at him, and feeling embarrassed by her parents' geniality which seemed to her dreadfully artificial. Blaise himself was the most self-possessed of the party. Drawn out by her father, he spoke of the war in Spain, and of Wellington, whom he seemed to regard with a mixture of reverence and amusement. He had a crisp, pleasant voice if you forgot about his face.

After dinner Pamela's mother sat her down firmly at the pianoforte. Blaise had said he was fond of music. Pamela stumbled through a Clementi sonata, hitting many wrong notes. This was not deliberate, though she did wonder whether a musical man would want a wife who played so badly. When she was finally allowed to escape upstairs, her mother came with her, leaving the men alone.

Now, though Pamela gloomily, I am going to get the most tremendous scolding.

But Mrs Stonebridge did not scold. Sitting in her dressing-room, with Pamela beside her, she said, 'You must listen very carefully to what I am going to tell you and not interrupt. I wanted to explain beforehand why we wanted to arrange this marriage for you, but Papa would not hear of it. He said it was unnecessary and I did not want to cause him any added pain. But never mind that now. The thing is, you see, we are not as rich as we used to be. In fact we are not rich at all. Papa has had some very heavy losses.'

'Losses!' exclaimed Pamela, forgetting not to interrupt. 'Do you mean at cards?'

'No, of course not! Who do you think he would find round here to stake thousands of pounds at whist? And he has never been a gamester. Unluckily he invested a very great sum of money in a London banking house which failed. It was a most respectable concern and Papa was in no way to blame. Everything seemed so promising at the time, but when Bonaparte escaped from Elba a great many commercial ventures were ruined.'

'But why, Mama? We beat him in the end.'

'Yes, but not immediately. His hundred days of freedom claimed many innocent victims, and the victory of the eighteenth of June came too late for companies that had been bankrupt in the spring. It is very hard to understand, but there is nothing to be done. The whole of Papa's investment has gone. We shall have to live very differently from now on. Sell this house and move into somewhere small and convenient, where we can manage with two or three servants.'

'Sell Crewse!' repeated Pamela, aghast.

'I'm afraid so. I shall not mind for myself,' said Mrs Stonebridge resolutely. 'Or for Papa. At our age we shall be happier living very quietly without the burden of a large establishment and much entertaining. On what we shall have, we could live in easy retirement for the rest of our lives. It is your future which is our chief anxiety.' Mrs Stonebridge paused as though expecting some comment, though perhaps not the one she received. Pamela had been doing mental arithmetic.

'It must be nearly two years since Papa lost all this money. Why is it only now we have to change our way of life? Why have you only just begun to talk of being poor and selling Crewse?'

'Well, for a long time we went on hoping that a good deal of Papa's investment might be recovered, but sadly it was not so. And we had another reason. You remember your godmother died during the winter?'

'Of course I remember. She left me a thousand pounds. I thought it very kind of her.' An idea flashed into Pamela's mind. 'Was it my godmother who

wanted to arrange a match between me and her—what
was he? Her nephew?'

'Her great-nephew. No, I don't think she ever
thought of that. You know, she was my very old
friend. We were girls together and she never had any
children, poor Mary. Or any close connections except
a much older sister who married into the Cressinder
family. The late Lord Blaise was Mary's nephew,
though they were very much of an age. She held him
and his heir in the greatest dislike and was determined
not to leave them a penny of her large fortune. Instead
she told me she intended to leave it all to you, her
favourite godchild.'

'To me?' repeated Pamela, staring.

'She was under no obligation to do so, and I
suppose we were wrong and foolish to take her
generosity as a settled thing. At least we never raised
your hopes. And it did comfort us a great deal, after
the failure of the bank, to believe that you would be
well provided for.

'I never told her of Papa's losses, and, by the time
she died, she had changed her will, which she had
every right to do. She had met the new Lord Blaise,
whom she had not seen since his childhood. He had
distinguished himself in the Army and turned out so
very differently from his father and brother. He was
her own flesh and blood. It was only natural that she
should decide to make him her heir. He seems to be
a very pleasant young man and to think just as he
ought. He has been in correspondence with Papa and
he is most anxious to marry and settle down. He
knows he displaced you in his great-aunt's will and
there is something truly chivalrous in his wishing to
make you an offer. I'm sure you must agree.'

Pamela did not agree. She thought he must be mad, until it struck her that it might be difficult for him, looking as he did, to find a girl who was willing to accept him. A marriage of convenience arranged at a distance was perhaps the best he could hope for.

'I dare say he means well,' she said, 'But surely I am not obliged to accept the first man who offers for me?'

'That is just the point. I expect you think we are being very worldly and even tyrannical in urging you towards this marriage, but we have been so anxious about your future. Papa is most apprehensive about what will become of you if you don't accept Blaise. He is afraid that with only a thousand pounds and living in the style we shall now be reduced to, you may never marry anyone at all.'

As Pamela did not really believe this, she answered quite cheerfully, 'That doesn't signify. I shan't care if I don't marry.'

'It would be a great pity,' said her mother, taking her hand. 'And you still don't understand, my love. I said Papa and I will be able to live comfortably on what we can save from the wreck—the funds will be ample to last our time. But you are only seventeen; you may live another sixty years. It is that thought which is torturing Papa, making him positively ill. I know he blames himself for losing your birthright, though indeed it was not his fault. If only you could bring yourself to marry this young man, it would make all the difference. Don't you think you could learn to like him?'

'He is so ugly, Mama. I cannot bear to look at him. How do you suppose he got that terrible scar?'

'In a cavalry charge at Waterloo,' said her mother quietly.

I might have known, thought Pamela, ashamed of her squeamishness and at the same time resentful, for she saw what she ought to do.

She was very sorry for her father. She wanted to spare him the distress that was undermining his health, and, though she struggled not to blame him for the change in their fortunes, she understood how bitterly he must be blaming himself. But it was the thought of her mother that really racked her conscience. Poor Mama, not merely leaving her old home and coming down in the world, but having to share her altered life with a man who grew more and more frail and difficult as he grew more despondent. And having me on her hands as well, Pamela admitted. For she would be part of this depressing household if she didn't marry Blaise, and, although she believed she could stand up to poverty better than her parents, she was not nearly so sure that she could endure her father's moods or what they would do to her mother.

They talked for some time longer before she went to bed, her problems unresolved, her mind a jumble of uncertainties.

In the morning she was still bedevilled by indecision. She went out early, wanting to be alone, and indulging sad thoughts about leaving the home where she had lived all her life, for she would have to do that, whatever happened.

She was standing at the top of the ha-ha, gazing mournfully at the primroses on the bank below, when she saw Lord Blaise coming towards her. He saw her too, stopped for a moment and then came on.

'Good morning, Miss Stonebridge.'

'Good morning, my lord,' she said, addressing him for the first time.

He stood beside her, looking rather grim; perhaps he couldn't help it. The confidence of yesterday and the easy, light manner had deserted him.

After a pause he said, 'I hope our first encounter didn't entirely turn you against me.'

'No, of course not. I'm sure you didn't burst into my room on purpose.' Blushing scarlet at her own ineptitude, she added, 'Those doors on the landing are quite stupid. Visitors can never find their way.'

'Well, perhaps I should apologise for that too, but I really meant our very first encounter, when I nearly knocked you down in the lane.'

Until then she had not been sure if he had recognised her.

Indignation returning, she said, 'You were driving too fast and you shouted at me.'

'I beg your pardon. I gave myself a bad scare when I saw you so close to the horses. That was why I shouted. And you took such an instant dislike to me that you went off somewhere and hid, and I believe you were hoping to avoid meeting me altogether.'

Pamela went on staring at the primroses. She felt very uncomfortable. He had guessed the truth, which must have been fairly obvious, but did he think she had simply disliked his bad driving and his bad manners or had he understood how repulsive she found that honourable scar?

Suddenly she thought she knew why he had decided to choose a wife in this old-fashioned way. She and her family were to accept him unseen. She thought this was a mean trick to play, yet at the same time she knew it was cruel and unjust that any man should be rejected because he had been wounded fighting for his country.

'I'm very sorry,' she whispered, not explaining what she meant.

'Now we have both made amends, may I come straight to the point and ask you to marry me? It is not very romantic, I know, but I promise to cherish and take care of you, and do everything I can to make you happy. Will you trust me to mean what I say?'

'Yes,' she said, and apparently she had said yes to both his questions.

She was on his good side, so she could not see the scar. He did not attempt to kiss her but simply took her hand in a firm, cool grasp. When they went in to breakfast, they told her parents they were engaged.

CHAPTER TWO

'So HERE we are at last,' said Blaise, jumping down from the carriage and himself lowering the steps before helping his bride to climb out.

Pamela was tired and almost dizzy after so many hours of swinging and bumping over seventy miles of cross-country roads. They had been married that morning, and, after a not very festive wedding breakfast and some tearful farewells, they had set out for Mallowdown, the ancestral home of the Cressinder family. They were not to have a wedding tour, at which Pamela was slightly relieved. Settled in their own house, it would not be so necessary to keep up a pretence of honeymooning bliss.

She gazed about her in the soft green light of a May evening. She had known that Mallowdown was several hundred years old, but was a little surprised by the castellated skyline, the spiky, ornamental turrets and general air of top-heavy grandeur which had appealed to the taste of a Jacobean Cressinder who had sensibly married the only daughter of a London goldsmith.

The main part of the house seemed to her uncomfortably shut in between two projecting wings which faced each other across a paved court. The heavily carved stonework was broken up by innumerable windows, all rather small and narrow.

There was a crowd of servants on the front steps, bobbing and staring at their new mistress. Blaise presented various old retainers to her and then led her on into the great hall.

This was an enormous gloomy apartment with a north aspect and a stone floor. Hanging on the wall were the antlers of a great many horned beasts, some fierce-looking ancient weapons and a series of huge horse paintings by Wootton.

'Gothic, isn't it?' he said. 'Literally so. I did try to prepare you. Well, it's not all as bad.'

He conducted her into a warren of smaller rooms, many of them richly decorated with plasterwork and tapestry, though all somewhat low and sombre. The massive furniture, though rather later than the house, was old enough to seem out of date.

Pamela's heart sank. She liked reading about the past and had felt a spark of interest when she had heard she was going to live in such a historic old place, but there was something alien here, a cold sense of neglect which had nothing to do with poverty. The Cressinders had never been poor. It was, she realised later, the atmosphere of a house where there had been no domestic affection for a great many years.

The two best rooms were on the first floor, the drawing-room having started life as a Jacobean great chamber and the huge dining-room adapted from a long gallery.

Here, after a short delay, the bride and bridegroom sat down to dinner without changing, watched over by rows of Cressinder ancestors in ruffs and Cavalier lovelocks and powdered wigs.

'Disapproving of our barbarous manners,' commented Blaise. 'But I didn't see why you and I should waste time dressing up for each other tonight.'

The end of the evening loomed alarmingly ahead. Perhaps he guessed what she was thinking. He sent the servants out of the room, saying he would wait on her ladyship himself.

Then, while preparing to carve a roast duck, he remarked casually, 'I shan't disturb you if you want to sleep off the effects of the journey. I shall quite understand.'

So she might gain a reprieve. But what would be the point? Better get it over.

'It is very thoughtful of you, my lord, but I shall be perfectly restored after this good dinner.'

'You don't have to call me that.'

She took a sip of wine and choked nervously. 'What am I to call you? Blaise?'

'I'd prefer Richard. I've been plain Richard Cressinder most of my life and I never expected to inherit.'

She had called him Richard once already, making her vows that morning. She had promised to love, honour and obey him. But she didn't love him, so surely she had done a terrible thing in perjuring herself so that she could get a rich husband, be called 'my lady' and live in this horrible house. She forgot the unselfish motives that had driven her to accept Blaise for the sake of her parents, feeling only that she was being false and mercenary. False especially to Ben, whose face seemed to hover in front of her as in a vision. He had been desperately hurt yet uncomplaining, which had made the haunting sadness in his eyes harder to bear. Beyond this inconvenient presence and across the shimmer of candle-light was the stranger she had married.

By the time she went up to bed she was extremely
nervous. Blaise—no, Richard, she must remember
that—escorted her as far as her bedroom door and
said he would join her later.

The room was large and formal with a canopy of
crimson cut velvet over the immense bed. It was not
the room his father had occupied; Richard had told
her so in a way that was obviously meant to reassure
her. She supposed the late Lord Blaise had shared his
bed with a good many highly improper companions.

Her new dresser, Toller, was waiting for her, an
experienced servant whom her mother had engaged
to look after her. She twittered about with soap and
scent and combs and one of the fine lawn night-
dresses that was part of Pamela's trousseau. She meant
well but they had only met a few days before and she
would behave as though this were an occasion of great
joy and celebration—which, of course, it should have
been.

Pamela slid down between the cold sheets, not
knowing what to expect. Naturally she knew what
Richard had to do before they could be properly
married and she could give him an heir. It was the
preliminaries which baffled her, the fear of not
behaving just as she ought. Mama had simply told
her she must be submissive, which did not seem quite
enough. She had a friend at home, a young woman
her parents considered fast. Fanny, after meeting
Richard once, had giggled excitedly and said that
Pamela was in luck; Blaise was an accomplished lover,
you could tell that a mile off.

What Fanny and Pamela did not understand, their
heads full of Gothic novels, was that in ordinary life
a man of the world went for pleasure to experienced

women who knew how the game should be played and who had no fears or uncertainties needing special consideration. Deflowering virgins had been no part of Richard Cressinder's education.

So that when he came in, tall and daunting in a dressing-gown of dark blue silk, she had no idea that he was almost as nervous as she was.

He leant over the bed as though to kiss her. She saw his scarred cheek very close for the first time. It was like a fine tear that had been cobbled together with coarse thread. She held her breath, half shutting her eyes. Then he changed his mind and straightened up, snapping out the candles before he climbed into bed.

Pamela lay rigid in the darkness, perfectly acquiescent as she had been told, yet innocently creating a barrier of tension that made any real exchange of tenderness impossible.

After the first painful episode, he said, 'I'm sorry I hurt you. It will be better next time.'

Next time, she thought miserably. Night after night for years and years and years. She went to sleep on the extreme edge of the bed and woke up in the early hours to find she was crying. She thought she'd been dreaming of Ben.

She could hear Richard's even breathing and dared not move about for fear of disturbing him. Next time she woke she was alone in the great bed and the room was full of sunlight.

Presently Toller came in, bringing her breakfast on a tray. She was full of smiles and sly curiosity. Pamela drank a cup of coffee and said she would get up, wanting to escape from Toller and the bedroom about equally.

Downstairs she met the butler, who told her that his lordship was in the walnut room and offered to show her the way. Pamela thanked him. She thought it would sound odd to refuse. Richard apparently used this panelled room off the great hall for conducting business and writing letters. He was sitting at a knee-hole desk covered with papers and there was an estate map on the wall.

He stood up as she came in. 'Good morning. I didn't expect you down so soon.'

'I'm sorry. Am I interrupting you? Shall I go away?'

'No, of course not,' he said quickly, not quite looking at her. 'I was just going out. Would you like to come?'

'Oh, yes, please. I should.'

It was warmer outside than indoors; she did not need a shawl. They walked right round the peculiar Jacobean mansion and Richard explained that the parterre of little interwoven hedges, now much overgrown, was a hundred years old and had been copied from the garden at Versailles.

'I'm going to root it out,' he said. 'I suppose I ought to get Repton to remodel the whole place, only I'm afraid he'd make me cut down the avenue and turn the canal into a lake.'

The canal was not one of the modern sort for transporting goods by boat; it was a narrow sheet of ornamental water with a still unbroken surface which reflected the sky like a mirror. Though it was too artificial for the fashions of today, Pamela thought it pretty and restful, and, when she said so, he seemed pleased.

So long as they were walking about the garden, concentrating on things they could see, they were able to talk to each other without much strain. When they returned to the house Pamela felt an awkwardness stealing over them both.

Richard wanted her to decide which of several rooms she would like to take over for everyday use, the upstairs drawing-room being kept for best occasions. There was the so-called Spanish parlour, where the walls were hung with gilded leather, the summer parlour, or, leading out of it, the green salon. Which would she prefer?

'I don't know,' she said stupidly, not caring for any of them very much.

'It's a pity you can't feign a little more interest,' he said roughly. 'You don't like anything here, do you? Apart from the canal. Throwing cold water is what you excel at.'

Pamela felt herself turning slowly scarlet. She knew that what he said was partly true, yet she was doing her best and she did not think she could survive much unkindness at present.

Richard had gone to stare out of the window. Standing with his back to her, he asked, 'Who is Ben?'

She began to tremble. 'I—I don't know what you mean.'

'Of course you do. You were crying for him in bed last night when you thought I was asleep.'

'I wasn't,' she retorted, and then remembered waking in tears. 'At least, if I was, it was all a dream and it cannot signify. There was never anything wrong between us.'

'I'm sure there wasn't.'

He spoke with a certainty which even in her present agitation she found slightly galling. Her total inexperience must be so plain to him.

He was still standing in the window, but he turned to look at her.

'That long-legged boy, the parson's son—he's called Ben, isn't he?'

Pamela did not answer. They had met only once, after church on the Sunday of Richard's first visit to Crewse. Poor Ben had hung about, tongue-tied, not cutting at all a dashing figure.

'Well, that's a relief,' Richard was saying, drawing the right conclusion from her silence. 'I was afraid I might have come between you and a man you seriously hoped to marry. But that schoolboy! It was your first little flirtation, I imagine. One takes these things to heart at seventeen. Even so, you must have known it wouldn't do.'

'He's not a schoolboy, he's up at Oxford,' muttered Pamela.

At that moment they heard a pair of horses clopping up the avenue.

'Who the devil can be calling on us today?' demanded Richard in a voice of grievance. 'What a display of vulgar curiosity. They might have left us to ourselves a little longer.'

'So that we could continue with our delightful billing and cooing?' enquired Pamela, suddenly made brave by her resentment.

Richard gave her a glance of pure astonishment, as though he had been bitten by the spaniel which lay adoring at his feet. Then a smart carriage slid past the window and his expression changed.

'Oh, it's Decima—Mrs Strang. That's different. I told you about her, she's our nearest neighbour. She promised she would call very soon.'

Pamela tried to remember. He had said that unluckily there were no suitable friends for her in their own village, but that the Strangs at Bourne House, three miles away, would make her very welcome. Mrs Strang in particular was just the sort of friend she needed: young, agreeable, gifted, the mother of two small children, a general favourite, everything that was charming.

She waited apprehensively for the arrival of this paragon. She felt she herself was looking very plain, still hot and red from the altercation with Richard. When the butler came in to ask whether she was at home to Mrs Strang, she dared not say no, which was just as well, for the lady came straight in behind him.

'Lady Blaise, I do hope you will forgive me. It is shockingly presumptuous of me to walk in on you like this. I did want to be sure you are not too uncomfortable in this old barrack. I am only doing what Richard's sister would do if he had one.' Mrs Strang paused long enough to shake hands with the bridegroom. 'How do you do, my dear Richard? I am glad to be one of the first to wish you joy.'

She was in her late twenties, just under middle height, with a clear musical voice, pretty features and wide-open eyes shining with good health and confidence. Although she was in the grey and lavender of half-mourning, she was remarkably elegant and not only in the way she dressed. There was a grace and finish about her figure and movements which made her quite uncommon.

'We are delighted to see you, Dessy,' said Richard with enthusiasm. 'Are we not, my dear?'

'Oh, yes, delighted,' said Pamela, adding awkwardly, 'Do take a chair, ma'am.'

Mrs Strang seated herself and looked around. 'Is this the room you have settled on for general use? It is just as depressing as the others; there is not much to choose between them.'

Hearing her own opinion confirmed, Pamela's heart warmed towards Mrs Strang. She shot Richard a challenging glance and he had the grace to laugh and come off his high horse.

'It seems you have an ally,' he admitted. 'I must tell you, Decima, that Pamela doesn't like these rooms any more than you do. But I don't see how we are to improve them overnight.'

Decima Strang was beginning to make suggestions when one of the footmen came in to say that Mr Graves, the land steward, wanted to speak to his lordship urgently. Richard excused himself and went out, leaving the women alone together.

'He does mean to have the house done over for you,' said Decima Strang immediately, 'and he understands what is needed in the more important rooms and how to preserve his family treasures. What he can't see is the proper way to introduce modern comforts without spoiling the effect. Very few men can. Least of all one who has spent the last ten years living in a tent.'

Pamela was struck by this reference to Richard's life in the Army. 'I suppose he was never here after he grew up?'

'Hardly at all. I'm afraid the late Lord Blaise was not a very good father. His character had a fatal effect on poor Tom, whose character was so unstable. He should have succeeded, you know, only he was killed in a driving accident six weeks before the old man suffered an apoplectic stroke.'

'How long ago did Richard's mother die?'

It was something Pamela had not yet managed to ask.

'About twenty-five years, I think. Richard was six at the time and Tom eight.'

Poor little boys, Pamela thought. No wonder the house has such an unloved feeling.

'I hope,' Mrs Strang was saying seriously, 'that you will make a point of seeing Richard goes regularly to church.'

'Doesn't he always? He did when he was with us at Crewse.'

'So I should suppose. And, while he was commanding his regiment, I think he set an example. But I am not convinced that he goes every Sunday here—we are not in the same parish and I don't care to ask. Now you are married, Lady Blaise, it is for you to see that he does everything in his power to restore his family's credit, which became sadly tarnished in his father's time.'

Pamela could not imagine herself making Richard go to church if he didn't want to, so she was relieved when Decima went back to talking about the house, with generous offers of help and advice which Pamela appreciated.

Decima left soon afterwards, and, when Richard came back, he found Pamela moving chairs about in the summer parlour and trying to banish a very ugly vase to a dark corner in the passage. He groaned, and said he supposed Decima was going to encourage her in turning the place upside-down, but he was clearly in a good temper.

'I knew you would like her,' he said with satisfaction.

'Yes, she is very kind.' Something was puzzling Pamela. 'Has she always lived in this neighbourhood?'

'No, she comes from Devonshire. She was born Decima Fabian. You are wondering, perhaps, how it is we use Christian names. I was at school with her brother George and I often spent holidays with the Fabians at Aldercombe. It was not always convenient for my father to have me at home. So when she married Hubert Strang—he is her cousin, by the way—we already knew each other very well. Do you want that table there, or would you rather have it under the window?'

The stiffness between them had worn off, thanks to the timely arrival of Mrs Strang.

CHAPTER THREE

WHEN Sunday came, Richard took it for granted that they were both going to church, only saying that he hoped Pamela wouldn't mind being gaped at by the whole congregation. As the Cressinder pew was in a side chapel, surrounded by family tombs and monuments, the congregation could not see the new Lady Blaise very well, and, if the unblinking stony eyeballs of her husband's ancestors were a little unnerving, at least they could not embarrass her.

Next day Richard drove her over to Bourne House in his curricle to return Decima's call. The Strangs' fine classical house reminded Pamela of her old home. They both dated from the reign of George II, but Decima predictably had a more up-to-date outlook than Mrs Stonebridge.

Her light rosewood and satinwood furniture was set out boldly in the middle of the rooms, instead of being pushed back against the walls, sofas stood at right angles to fireplaces with sofa tables in front of them and lavishly draped curtains harmonised with Wedgwood urns.

They were hardly seated when some other callers arrived: Mr Carriswood, a local magistrate, with his wife and sister. Pamela soon gathered that the Carriswoods, together with the Cressinders and Strangs, were the three most considerable landowning families in the neighbourhood.

Mrs Carriswood, a formidable lady in her fifties, set about interrogating the bride, trying to assess exactly what her background had been.

The former Miss Stonebridge of Crewse Manor was perfectly able to hold her own in a conversation of this kind, but was rather at a loss when Miss Amelia Carriswood joined in, wondering archly how long she had known Lord Blaise and where they had met. These middle-aged people would probably look on a marriage of convenience as quite acceptable, but Pamela herself was deeply ashamed that her parents had handed her over to the first comer, a man who did not even care what she looked like. She was struggling for an answer when Richard himself came to her rescue.

'Were you ever acquainted with my great-aunt Lady Emden, ma'am?' he said to Miss Carriswood. 'Pamela was her goddaughter. It was through her that we were introduced.'

Which was true enough in its way.

Mr Strang now came to sit beside Pamela. He was an extremely tall, cadaverous man, quite old and not very interesting. She was disappointed in him—she would have expected Decima to have chosen better. But he was kind and easy to talk to in a dull sort of way and was clearly a devoted husband, his glance constantly turning to his vivacious wife with an admiration which must be very heart-warming, thought Pamela a little wistfully.

Richard had to prompt her when it was time to leave and this made her feel awkward.

Decima said, 'We have had no opportunity to talk. I will come and see you very soon.'

Mrs Carriswood also said that, of course, they would be calling at Mallowdown. 'I had intended to leave you in seclusion a little longer, Lady Blaise, but then I am old-fashioned. Married women nowadays seem eager to rush into society the moment the ring is on.'

This was said with a merry laugh which was meant to remove offence but didn't.

'Spiteful old cat,' commented Richard, as they drove away from Bourne House.

Pamela had thought that Mrs Carriswood was simply tilting against the younger generation, as old people so often did, but there was probably more to it than that. Very likely all the neighbours guessed, if they did not know for certain, that she and Richard were only too anxious to escape from the seclusion which must be so delightful to a couple truly in love.

As they bowled on down the avenue she caught sight of a small girl of eight or nine walking with a young woman in the park. Richard raised his hat and waved to them, and the child called out something and waved back.

'Who was that?' asked Pamela.

She knew it was not one of the Strangs' children, for she had heard all about little Hubie and Dessy, aged six and five.

'Alice Fabian, Decima's niece. The Strangs are bringing her up. The girl with her is her governess, Miss Stevens.'

'Is her mother dead?'

'Divorced,' said Richard, negotiating a difficult bend.

This was startling. The Stonebridges had never been remotely connected with anyone who was divorced.

'Did you know her?'

'Bel Fabian? Certainly. She's Islington's daughter, an accredited beauty though always very wild. She got into a number of scrapes while George was serving in Spain and after he came home she eloped. That was when Decima took on Alice, like the Good Samaritan she always is. Poor George, he was out of luck. He had the kind of injuries that severely affected his health. Not, like mine, a mere scratch.'

A mere scratch, thought Pamela, looking straight ahead over the horses' ears and wondering guiltily whether Richard had guessed how she felt about that scar. Their physical contacts were so rare, embraces non-existent apart from those brief, compulsory moments of penance every night in the dark.

She had no idea whether Richard got any more pleasure from his conjugal rights than she did. The subject was never spoken of. In the daytime they were beginning to get on more easily together. He was kind and intelligent and he could be very amusing, especially when he spoke of his life in the Army.

At eighteen he had joined a famous hussar regiment, always known as the Scarlets, because of the blood-red sashes they wore in full dress, commemorating a particularly desperate action they had fought under Marlborough. Richard had served right through the Peninsular War and ended his career by commanding the regiment at Waterloo. She enjoyed listening to his stories and riding with him round the estate.

She felt illogically that married life would be quite pleasant if only one didn't have to be married.

And then, just as she was precariously adapting to the life she had to lead, she was faced by a new situation. It was not unexpected, though it took her by surprise, happening so quickly.

Richard had not made her fall in love with him, but he had instantly made her pregnant.

There was never any doubt, no need to wait a few weeks longer to be certain. Pamela was sick every morning and felt queasy most of the day. She felt different all over, bewildered. She was delighted she was going to have a baby and that Richard was so obviously pleased, but she had not realised she would feel so ill.

'Do I have to go on like this for nine months?' she asked Decima, who had come over to congratulate her.

'The first few weeks are often a little trying, but they will soon pass. The great thing is never to think too much about your health. All you need is fresh air with gentle exercise and plenty to occupy your mind, and you will soon find yourself perfectly comfortable.'

This was very well-meaning. Unfortunately it wasn't true. Pamela continued to be sick and presently she began to have intolerable migraine headaches which she had never suffered from before. She was a strong, active girl who had hardly ever been ill and she did not know how to cope with her ailments.

She felt very despondent and longed for her mother, who wrote her loving, sympathetic letters but was unable to come to her. Mr and Mrs Stonebridge were in the process of removing to Bath. They had not, after all, sold Crewse Manor; instead they had let it to a friend of Richard's who wanted a house in that part of the country. This was a great convenience, but all the difficulties of moving her invalid husband into a house in Queen's Parade made it impossible for Mrs Stonebridge to come to her daughter.

'I am sure Richard is taking good care of you,' she wrote. 'We had such a very attentive letter from him, full of your praises.'

Pamela was glad to hear it. Richard was gentle and thoughtful, but she did not think he liked people to be feeling out of sorts. It made him uncomfortable; he did not know what to do with himself in a sick-room.

But she would not complain, certainly not to Mama, who had added in her letter, 'How fortunate you are to have such a friend as Mrs Strang.'

Decima was a tower of strength; she rode or drove over nearly every day, taking endless trouble to raise Pamela's spirits and improve her surroundings.

So Pamela was disconcerted to find that she was beginning to be irritated by her dear friend's constant advice and the way she was taking over the management of everything at Mallowdown, giving orders to the servants as though she were in her own home and organising an open-air reception at which Richard and Pamela were to entertain their neighbours.

On this particular morning, Pamela felt worse than usual but dared not say so.

She got up and allowed herself to be dressed like a French fashion doll in bridal white and pearls, and then fainted away just as the first guests were going to be announced.

It was Hubert who caught her as she fell—naturally the Strangs had arrived early to lend their support. Dropping into a dark abyss, unable to see, speak or feel any physical sensation, Pamela could still hear. The invisible voices around her were eerily sharp.

'I thought as soon as I saw her that she looked extremely ill. I never saw anyone as pale.' This was Hubert.

'Nonsense,' declared Decima. 'She is suffering from an attack of nerves, that's all.'

'I don't know what she has to be nervous about,' said Richard.

Here Pamela sank into unconsciousness, and recovered later to find herself lying on her bed, while downstairs the party took place without her, Decima acting as deputy hostess.

Pamela was furious with herself. She, who had never fainted in her life, disdaining those who went in for fits of the vapours and other displays of female stupidity! Richard and Decima were very sympathetic, but she was convinced that they despised her and almost hated them for being so healthy and uncomprehending.

CHAPTER FOUR

'GOOD gracious, what do you want with all those grapes?' demanded Decima.

She was sitting with Pamela when the butler came in carrying a tray with a large china dish on it, piled high with swelling clusters of hothouse fruit, almost iridescent from the sweet-scented bloom that was still fresh on their green skins.

Decima went on without waiting for an answer, 'What can Jessel be about, sending in so many bunches? You had better pass on a message to the gardens, Thompson, telling him not to cut them all at once.'

Thompson was the butler. He bowed with the gravity of a bishop, but did not reply.

Pamela said defiantly, 'I like grapes and I have a craving for them at present. Put the dish down here, will you, Thompson? Thank you.'

She selected a bunch for herself and began to devour the grapes inelegantly, spitting out the skins and pips on to a plate.

'You cannot hope to keep up your strength if you live entirely on fruit,' commented Decima.

Pamela took no notice. It was now October, she was five months gone and no longer sick every day though she had plenty of other troubles: sensations of vertigo, swollen ankles, agonising cramps and continuing headaches. She had to get through this nightmare as best she could and the added irritation of Decima's good advice was something she could well do without. She went on silently working her way up her bunch of grapes from the tip to the stalk. At last Decima spoke again with her usual good humour.

'I hope you won't take it amiss, my dear Pamela,' she said in her pretty, musical voice, 'if I talk to you on a serious matter. You should make more effort to overcome your low spirits and take a more sensible attitude towards your condition. There is nothing out of the way in having a baby. All women are subject to some inconvenience and most of them, let me remind you, are not nearly so comfortably placed as you are. I am not thinking simply of the poor, who are often cold and hungry, but of the women in our own state of life. The wives of Army officers, for instance. Suppose you had married Richard when he was merely Colonel Cressinder, commanding a regiment of Hussars. You might have been trundling about the countryside from place to place, following the drum, or left to fend for yourself in some dingy lodging with no one to take care of you. That is how many ladies started their families during the war. I know how greatly Richard admired their stoicism. Don't you think you should try and show a little of the same spirit?'

Pamela was struck dumb. She had not felt so mortified since she was quite a small child and her nurse had scolded her for not eating up her mutton fat when so many little boys and girls were starving. Her sufferings were quite genuine, whatever Decima might suppose, and she did not think cramp or indigestion would be much worse in dingy lodging than it was in Richard's ancestral home. What she disliked most was the suggestion that she was putting on the airs of a fine lady.

At last she managed to say, in a strangled voice, 'Have you been discussing me with Richard?'

As Decima did not answer, Pamela immediately concluded that she had.

She said defensively, 'Do you think I am exaggerating my symptoms in order to amuse myself and make everyone feel sorry for me?'

'Certainly not, my dear. Only it is so easy, is it not, to fall into a habit of complaining without meaning to? I knew you would not mind my giving you a hint,' concluded Decima with a sweet, reassuring smile and a completely false idea of the effect she was having on her companion. She went on to talk cheerfully about something different.

After she had gone Pamela stamped about the room in a tearing rage, thumping the cushions to relieve her feelings. She would have liked to lie down on the floor and scream, only she was sure it would be bad for the baby.

She knew she was behaving stupidly and looking ridiculous, flushed and fat and plain, bursting out of her dress as though it had grown tighter since she put it on this morning. All her dresses seemed to do this now.

She was absently running her fingers through her curly red-gold hair, so that it looked like a bird's nest, when Thompson threw open the door and announced, 'Mrs Savage and Mrs Cantley, my lady.'

In came two very pretty young women whom she had never seen before, one dark and one fair.

'How do you do?' said Pamela uncertainly, feeling a perfect fright.

Who could they possibly be? She seemed to recall the names, but could not place them.

'Do forgive us for walking in on you, ma'am,' said the older visitor. She was the dark one. 'I am Eliza Savage and this is my sister-in-law Hebe Cantley. We are on our way to Winchester and could not resist calling to offer the colonel our congratulations. He said you would not mind if we came to look for you. He has taken Hector and Jack round to the stables.'

The colonel, thought Pamela. They meant Richard, of course, and now she remembered why she had heard their names.

'Do sit down,' she said, looking about her distractedly and noticing the plate covered with grape pips. 'I'm afraid this room is not very tidy. Your husbands are in Richard's old regiment, are they not?'

'Oh, yes, and how they miss him,' said the fair girl. 'Things are not at all the same without Colonel Richard. Lord Blaise, I mean.'

These, thought Pamela, were the kind of women Decima had been talking about earlier, come here by some malign coincidence to put her to shame. Making stilted conversation, she enquired about their families, and was pleased to discover they had not suffered such terrible hardships in the process of childbearing. Eliza's two daughters had been born at her parents' house in Yorkshire while she herself had gone last year to look after Hebe at the house the Cantleys had rented now the regiment was stationed at Hounslow.

'And when do you expect to be confined, Lady Blaise?' asked Eliza.

'Not until January. I shall be glad when it is over, for I feel perfectly horrid most of the time, and the worst of it is everyone thinks I am making a mountain out of a molehill. I certainly look like a mountain already.'

'I know exactly how you feel,' said Eliza sympathetically. 'Friends can be such a bunch of Job's comforters. And some pregnancies are far more difficult than others. I was miserably ill while I was carrying Maria, yet with Charlotte I never felt better, able to ride and dance all the way through.'

Pamela was charmed with this intelligent guest.

'You must be hoping to have a boy,' said Hebe. 'Eliza, do you think Lady Blaise would like you to do your wedding-ring test?'

This involved dangling a wedding-ring in front of a pregnant woman to see whether it gyrated in circles or swung like a pendulum. The first indicated a girl, the second a boy.

'Do let's try,' said Pamela. 'Does it work? I don't see how it can.'

'It has to do with electricity,' said Hebe, round-eyed.

Pamela was more mystified than ever.

Eliza took a pair of scissors and a spool of thread from her reticule, knotted a length of it through her ring and held it before Pamela's midriff as though she were performing some ancient rite. The ring refused to move in any direction unless Eliza gave it a shake. Hebe and Pamela then cried out that she was cheating. They did not learn anything about the sex of the baby but all laughed a great deal and were taken by surprise when Richard came in with Major Savage and Captain Cantley.

The captain was a very good-looking young man, as dark as his wife was fair. He was Eliza's brother.

Major Savage was older; he looked humorous and reliable.

They were clearly attached to Richard and he was in high spirits, telling Pamela that these very welcome visitors were going to stay to dinner and drive on to their destination by moonlight.

It was the pleasantest evening she had so far spent at Mallowdown. The old campaigners had so much to talk about, the wives almost as much as the men, for they had been everywhere with the regiment since the end of the war in Spain. Both had been in Brussels during that fatal June two years ago.

But Pamela was not made to feel left out. They all wanted to explain every reference to her, often capping each other's tall stories. Richard pretended to flirt with both Eliza and Hebe. Pamela, watching, realised how attractive he was to women and how they sparkled back at him, though it was all an innocent game.

She was not in the habit of looking directly at him, partly on account of the scar but mostly because she was embarrassed by the knowledge of her intimacy with this man who was really still a stranger. Now she saw the dark outline of his head, his broad shoulders, his clever, ravaged face as though through the eyes of other women and she felt a curious stab of regret. If only they could have met in happier circumstances, ventured into liking and admiration before there was any question of marriage, everything might have been different. As for the wound on his cheek, when he was in this mood it virtually disappeared.

It was very quiet in the Spanish parlour after the visitors had left. Richard went out to speed them on their way. When he came back he was still smiling.

'It does one good to see old friends. I hope our noisy party did not tire you.'

'Not in the least. I liked them all so very much.'

He sat down beside her. 'Whatever were you girls doing when we came in?'

'Trying to find out whether the baby is a boy. I know it sounds ridiculous.'

She explained about the ring. He was amused.

'And that dear little feather-brain Hebe thinks it has to do with electricity—she would! Though I don't suppose modern science would be any less effective than counting magpies.'

'No, and the magpies are never there to be counted. I don't believe in any of these fanciful ideas,' added Pamela, anxious not to sound silly.

'Not even the one about avoiding the sight of a man with a harelip—or a disfiguring scar?' Richard's voice had become cold and clipped. 'I thought you were a deal frightened about that.'

Pamela was appalled. 'You are mistaken,' she stammered, 'I wasn't aware—I didn't want you to think——'

He put a hand over hers. 'My dear child, I've known ever since our wedding day that you can hardly bear to look at me. If I hadn't been so slow-witted I'd have guessed at once, before we became engaged. I thought you were simply nervous and shy. And then we were married so soon, on account of your father's health. If I'd guessed the truth I'd never have gone through with it.'

'This is dreadful,' she said, almost in tears. 'How heartless I must have seemed. And wicked, when you had been so brave.'

'Oh, yes, heroic,' he agreed on a note of mockery. 'Those two scallywags this evening gave you a wonderful account of my exploits.'

'They have the greatest admiration for you,' she said seriously, 'and so do I.'

Impulsively she lifted her hand to touch his cheek and run her fingers along the seam of the scar. It no longer filled her with any revulsion. He said nothing, just took her hand and held it.

Once again she wondered why he had married her. Had she really suspected him of negotiating for an unknown bride at long distance because no girl who knew what he looked like would be willing to marry him? That was nonsense. He could still have taken his pick in spite of the scar. So why had he settled for a wife with so little to recommend her? Not merely a stranger but young, inept, unused to fashionable life and not even rich. Unless he was in love with someone else and didn't much care what his wife was like so long as she made no great demands on him.

And there was someone else, beautiful and charming and close at hand, someone whose ideas and plans always pleased him and who could do no wrong. Decima.

She wondered that she had never thought of this before.

'You're cold,' he said, feeling her shiver. 'I think you should go to bed.'

She was sleeping alone now; he had moved out of her bedroom soon after she became pregnant, and she had been thankful, tormented by sickness, indigestion and recently by excruciating cramp. So she was able to heave herself about without fear of waking him as she thought about him and Decima.

She did not suppose for a moment that they were lovers. Decima was far too good to do anything wrong. And Richard? Well, if Richard was not quite so good, Pamela felt instinctively that he would not behave as he did towards Decima if he had seduced her and they were carrying on a furtive intrigue. But a virtuous, unattainable love for a married woman, that was only too likely. Everyone behaving honourably and unselfish Decima doing her best to support and educate Richard's young bride and mould her into the sort of wife he needed. And I don't want to be moulded by her, thought Pamela crossly. Always being made to feel feeble and inferior. The worst of it is, I am inferior. I'll never be able to be anything else or stand on my own feet until I've had this baby. Even then I suppose I shall have a girl. I don't suppose I'm capable of giving Richard a son.

Here she was too modest. When the long months of waiting were over, she did not simply have a son.

She had twins.

CHAPTER FIVE

RICHARD was delighted with Pamela.

'How clever of you, my dearest girl,' he said in a voice full of tenderness and admiration, gazing down at her as she lay in bed, and at the two little creatures ensconced together in the same cradle while the estate carpenter hastily made a second.

They were as bald and red and hungry as fledgelings in a nest, on the small side, which was natural, but perfectly healthy. They were to be called Richard and Roland, both Cressinder family names.

'Can you tell them apart?' asked their father doubtfully. 'I can't. Not yet at any rate. I hope I shall later on.'

'Rich has this little mole on his wrist,' said Pamela. 'Do you see? So there will be no confusion over which is the heir.'

'How very fortunate. We shall not be obliged to put Roly into an iron mask.' Richard sounded perfectly serious but his eyes were dancing.

Pamela smiled back at him. She would not have thought it possible nine months ago that she could feel so comfortable with him and so content. The babies were going to make all the difference.

She was a little disappointed that she hadn't enough milk for them. It was considered the right thing nowadays for ladies to suckle their own infants—needless to say, Decima had fed hers. But Pamela was not going to be plagued by comparisons with Decima; she engaged a healthy wet-nurse, and, very soon after she recovered from her lying-in, they were all to move up to London for the season and so that Richard could attend the House of Lords.

The social life of the capital centred round the sessions of Parliament. Members of both Houses and everyone who aspired to be fashionable lived in London from February to July. The Blaises had stayed down in the country last year on account of their marriage, followed immediately by Pamela's difficult pregnancy, but Richard had a town house in Half Moon Street.

'And we have rented one in Albermarle Street, so we shall be even nearer neighbours than we are now,' Decima informed her with the pleased, confident smile of someone imparting good news.

'Are you going to be in town? I didn't know. You didn't go last year.' Pamela hoped she had kept the dismay out of her voice.

'No,' said Decima, 'because we were in mourning for Hubert's mother, if you remember, and it didn't seem right to be gadding about enjoying ourselves. And, to be perfectly truthful, Hubert does not greatly care for town life. But it all turned out for the best, because I was here and able to make myself useful when you needed me.'

It was hardly possible to go on resenting anyone who seemed so unsuspecting.

The Strangs actually set off before the Blaises, so Pamela was able to make all her own arrangements without supervision.

She was feeling very cheerful on a rainy afternoon towards the beginning of March, when she and Richard drove along Piccadilly in a smart new trav-

elling chariot with a coronet on the door and turned
into Half Moon Street. The babies and their nurse-
maids were in a second chaise immediately behind. A
full complement of servants had established themselves the day before and were waiting to greet them.

Pamela was pleased with the house. She had known
it would be in good repair, because it had been lent,
for the last two years, to some Cressinder relations
who had daughters to bring out.

They made a tour of inspection. The drawing-room
was hung with pale green damask, the shining chairs
and tables inlaid with ormolu. Standing in the window
was a handsome jardinière, lined with lead and planted
with spring flowers.

'Where did that come from?' Richard wondered.

There was a note poked in among the snowdrops.
Pamela picked it up and read it.

> To welcome you to your London home. I could
> not resist getting this for you; there does not
> seem to be one in the house. A bientôt. D.S.

'It's from Decima.'

'How very kind of her, she is always so thoughtful.
Let me see what she says.' He read the note and ex-
amined the jardinière with what Pamela considered
excessive admiration.

'You must write and thank her for it at once, today.'

'Yes, Richard,' said his wife meekly.

And she had hardly settled the babies and their at-
tendants in the nurseries high up at the top of the
house before he asked her whether she had remembered to write to Decima. She had a gloomy feeling
that she was still in the process of being moulded.

But London life was very different from the long
isolation of her pregnancy at Mallowdown. There were
so many other people to meet, so many things to do,
that it was easy to limit her encounters with Decima
or to plead a prior engagement if she became too
intrusive.

Pamela had to become acquainted with Richard's
aunt, Lady Brunard, who was going to present her at
one of the Drawing-Rooms. There were a lot of young
Brunards, male and female, all disposed to be
agreeable and uncritical, and of course Richard had
many other friends. Pamela was fully recovered by
now and she felt and looked extremely well. Her figure
was improved; she was not as thin as she had been.

The twins had added greatly to her status. No one
could recall any other peer whose wife had provided
him with two heirs within a year of their marriage.
That was a triumph and she made the most of it.

Many girls of her own age had come to London for
their first season, beset by fears of failure, dreading
the disgrace of not being danced with at balls, inclined
to lose their hearts to men who never looked twice at
them, or worse, men who pursued them with enthusiasm but never made them an offer.

Pamela was spared all this and was thankful for it.
She could hardly remember what it was she had felt
for poor Ben Watney. She was far better off with
Richard even though they were not in love. Or perhaps
because they were not in love, she told herself with a
carefully cultivated cynicism. They were good friends
now and she would never need to feel threatened or
disturbed by Richard's attachment to Decima provided she herself was not made into a sacrificial victim
on the altar of high-minded infatuation. Sooner or

later she might have to make this plain to Richard, but she hesitated. Easygoing as he was, there was something a little daunting about him when he was thwarted. She could be afraid of him.

In any case, she could hardly object, before her first dinner party, when Decima threw herself into organising the whole affair with tireless energy, so that Pamela would have a great success. It was, as Richard kept pointing out, so very kind of her.

The menu and the guest-list were discussed at length, the flowers and what Pamela was going to wear.

As to the last item, Decima disapproved of her choice in the friendliest possible way. On the morning of the party she sent round Alice Fabian and her governess with a note full of last-minute suggestions.

'What are you going to wear at your dinner, Lady Blaise?' asked Alice, a thin, pale child, rather small for nine, with straight dark hair.

'Would you like to come and see?'

'Oh, yes, please.'

They went upstairs to Pamela's dressing-room. She opened her new hanging wardrobe and took out a tunic of soft pink gauze which floated over a satin slip almost the colour of ripe apricots.

'Isn't it beautiful?' breathed Alice reverently.

She was not a very experienced judge. Pamela glanced at the governess, a quiet, rather enigmatic young woman who somehow managed to look elegant in spite of the dull clothes she was obliged to wear.

'What do you think, Miss Stevens?'

'It is a charming dress, ma'am, and that colour suits you perfectly.'

'Mrs Strang thinks it clashes with my hair. I know they always say red-haired women should not wear pink, but I don't consider myself a true red any longer, though I was as a child.'

'Even if you were still, that dress would become you. With your skin you could wear anything. One of my brothers is a painter and he says ladies are too easily frightened out of choosing the very colours they could wear most effectively.'

'That is the kind of encouragement I need. Now I can do as I please with a clear conscience.'

Miss Stevens said thoughtfully, 'Some women have no eye for colour. They play safe and think they are being fashionable when they look just like everyone else.'

Pamela felt certain she was speaking of her employer. She could hardly say more in front of Alice. In any case there was a conventional barrier. The Strangs' governess could not expect to exchange confidences with Lady Blaise, however enjoyable it might have been for them both.

And I must try not to be so petty, Pamela told herself that evening when she was dressing for the great occasion. Decima can't eat me, even if she doesn't like my dress.

Toller had finished doing her hair. Pamela stood up and surveyed her shimmering reflection in the cheval-glass as Richard came in to find her. For a moment he did not speak and she wondered whether he considered the daring choice of colour had been a mistake.

'What do you think?' she asked a little nervously.

'You look stunning,' he said with conviction. 'How lucky I am to have such a beautiful wife!'

They went down to the drawing-room together in the best of spirits.

Pamela had been afraid that the Strangs would arrive early so that Decima could make a lot of last-minute alterations. If she had meant to do so she was defeated by Richard's aunt, Lady Brunard, who had been arriving early at dinner parties all her life. She was an amiable woman without a great deal of social perception, and it had probably never crossed her mind to wonder why her hosts and hostesses were often slightly out of breath when they greeted her. She had her husband with her and an unmarried son and daughter, so that when the Strangs arrived a few minutes later Decima was not able to comment on the pink dress.

The other guests assembled. They were a large party, eighteen in all, and soon the moment came that Pamela had been dreading. Somehow everyone had to be paired off, shepherded down a flight of stairs to the dining-room on the ground floor, and persuaded to sit where she wanted them at the long table. This was all the more difficult because it had to look easy. At official gatherings there was a great deal of etiquette and ceremony; at private parties everything was supposed to happen quite naturally without a lot of fuss. Yet none of the Blaises' aristocratic guests would care to be placed lower down the table than their rank demanded, while husbands and wives did not expect to find themselves put next to each other by mistake. Pamela touched wood and hoped for the best and by some miracle everyone ended up where they were supposed to.

She gazed down the fully extended table towards Richard at the far end. He seemed a very long way off. The tablecloth was almost hidden by painted Sèvres china in every shape and size. Glass glittered and silver gleamed against the starched whiteness. She need not worry about the food provided by their excellent French cook, but were the dishes being offered quickly enough and was everybody talking to an agreeable neighbour? It was dreadful when someone got stranded between two pockets of conversation; the hostess was supposed to put matters right—but how?

'Don't torment yourself,' said a voice beside her, 'you are doing very well.'

She turned to Lord Charles Everard. The younger son of a duke, he was entitled to the place on her right and she was glad of this, for although he was inclined to be a dandy, he had a reassuring smile and she liked him and his wife as much as any couple she had met in London.

'You must forgive me if I seem a little *distraite*. This is our first dinner party.'

'Yes, I know. Decima Strang told Emily.'

She would, thought Pamela, irritated. I expect she has gone round London telling everyone that she has had to organise this dinner because I have no idea how to go on, and how badly I dress and how hopeless I was when I was carrying the twins. She knew she must not show annoyance.

She said, 'Lady Charles is such a very good hostess.'

'Yes, she is, isn't she?' Charles Everard agreed eagerly. 'She is one of those remarkable people who does everything well. Not that she ever gives herself airs—which is what one dislikes so much in accomplished people. Emily was dreadfully apprehensive when we first began to entertain. We both were. We used to imagine that all the fires would smoke, or the butler fall down drunk.'

What a delightful man he is, she thought, and how fond of his wife. She was sorry when she had to switch her attention to her other neighbour, but by now she had gained confidence and was able to enjoy herself.

The first course of fish, meat and vegetables was removed. The second course consisted of poultry and game, various spiced savouries as well as creams and pastries. When these had been eaten the cloth was withdrawn and a beautiful dessert service, with Italian scenes painted on every plate, was laid on the shining mahogany. Hothouse fruit and sweetmeats were set down, decanters placed in silver coasters, and Pamela became nervous again, because the moment was approaching when she would have to collect the eyes of the ladies and whisk them all upstairs, leaving the gentlemen to their port and brandy.

She watched carefully to make sure that everyone had finished eating and was just about to rise when she saw that Richard's cousin Anna Brunard had just began to peel a peach. She had been talking about music with great animation to the man beside her and had not noticed that she was lagging behind the rest of the fruit eaters. Anna was twenty-two, very musical but no great beauty. If the ladies rose to leave now she would be made to look foolish and conspicuous, and this would annoy her father, who had a very sharp tongue. Pamela decided that she must wait. She went on talking to Lord Charles.

A minute later Decima, three places beyond him, leant forward and said quite audibly to Pamela, 'I think it's time you took the ladies upstairs.'

Pamela felt herself growing scarlet with mortification. It was outrageous to be treated in her own house like a child who didn't know how to behave. Especially when she had been trying to act as a considerate hostess. Out of the corner of her eye she saw Anna hastily hiding the remains of her peach under her knife and fork. There was nothing for Pamela to do but stand up, cast a random glance toward the ladies nearest her, and say as steadily as she could, 'Shall we leave the gentlemen to their wine?'

Everyone was up in an instant, as though they had all been waiting for Decima to tell her what to do. She got herself and the other women out of the room but could not manage to speak to anyone until Lady Charles Everard caught up with her on the stairs.

'I do admire your dress, Lady Blaise,' she said in a friendly, unaffected voice. 'In fact, I have been telling your husband he ought to get Lawrence to paint you in it. The effect would be very striking.'

Pamela could not help thinking that at the moment her appearance must be striking indeed, her hot skin clashing with both her dress and her hair. But she was sure the compliment was sincere, and that in its way was a triumph over Decima, for Lady Charles was herself extremely elegant.

Regaining her composure, she was able to laugh and say, 'I'm not at all sure whether Sir Thomas will consent to paint me at all. Fair hair is so very much out of fashion.'

After that she was able to get through the rest of the evening. The men did not stay long in the dining-room and when they were all reassembled there were cards and music and conversation, and everyone seemed to think the party a success; at any rate they stayed long enough.

At the other end, when all the other guests had gone, the Strangs remained to talk over the evening with Richard and Pamela.

'I think that went off very well,' said Richard with satisfaction. 'You were a capital hostess, my love, and everyone kept saying how pretty you were. Not that I needed telling.'

'I should hope not,' said Decima, smiling. 'Pamela is in great good looks. And I must admit I was wrong about that dress, my dear. The colour is extremely becoming to you.'

Pamela had been bottling up her anger for two hours and was not going to be appeased by this belated generosity.

She said coldly, 'I know you like giving me good advice, but please do not give it so publicly in future. When you told me it was time to leave the table, I felt as though I were about six years old and had just spilt my bread and milk.'

'Good gracious!' exclaimed Decima. 'I did not mean to upset you. I simply thought you were so interested in your conversation with Lord Charles that you had forgotten what you had to do next.'

'I know what you thought, and let me tell you that once again you were mistaken. I had just seen that Anna Brunard had started eating a peach, and if I got up then she would be made to look silly and her father would be horrid to her later. I thought it was a part of good manners to save people from embarrassment, not to be always scoring off them and holding them up to ridicule.'

Decima looked completely taken aback. This was a Pamela she had never seen—the girl who had been quite prepared to fight against her marriage to Richard Blaise and who had only given way in face of a family catastrophe. When Decima had known her first she had been forlorn, confused, almost stunned by the destruction of her happiness, and the rest of that year she had felt too wretchedly ill to show any sign of independence.

Richard glanced from one to the other, mystified. From his end of the dining-room table he had not heard Decima officiously prompting Pamela. He only knew that his wife had just been extremely rude to the friend who had been so kind to her and who was, incidentally, a guest in their own house.

He said, sharply, 'You are not to speak to Decima like that. I don't understand what you are complaining of, but in any case there is no call to be uncivil.'

'I was not uncivil. I was simply pointing out that I do not care to be made to look a fool.'

'My dear, you are exaggerating. No one would have thought the worse of you if you had forgotten to make a move from the dining-room. They all knew you were giving your first dinner party,' said Decima with maddening forbearance.

'Yes, because you ran about telling everyone,' Pamela pointed out.

Decima looked as though she was going to remonstrate, when Hubert said anxiously, 'It is getting very late. We shall outstay our welcome, Dessy, if we go on talking too long.'

He gave his wife an imploring, slightly sheeplike glance. He hated arguments.

'Yes, it is high time we went home. I can see Pamela is over-tired.'

Decima allowed herself to be led away. Richard showed them out without summoning the butler. Pamela could hear their voices retreating down the stairs. She thought he was apologising.

She stood alone in the drawing-room, which seemed uncomfortably large and bright now everyone had gone. When Richard came back he was looking decidedly grim.

'What the devil do you mean by behaving so badly to Decima?'

'Why didn't you ask what the devil she meant by behaving so badly to me?'

'Don't talk nonsense. All she did was try and help you out of a difficulty, and if you didn't need help, there was no need to lose your temper and make such a scene. I can't think what came over you.'

Pamela was not entirely sure herself. With one half of her mind she knew the dining-room episode had been trivial and ridiculous, but with the other half she felt it was essential to stand up for herself before she was entirely smothered by Decima's benevolent despotism. Richard did not seem able to see this—but then Richard was blinded by his infatuation for the wretched woman.

Breathing rather hard, Pamela said, 'I know it sounds petty. I could have taken a hint from anyone else, your aunt for instance, but I am sick to death of being put in my place and patronised by wonderful Decima who knows what is best about everything. Haven't you noticed that she can never bear to be in the wrong?'

'Well, that's a lie!' he retorted. 'She admitted just now she was wrong in advising you not to wear that dress. She said how well it suited you. She's always very generous to other women.'

'Oh, yes,' said Pamela, annoyed by this argument. 'She is generous in small things. She is sorry she said I should not wear a pink dress, but she'll never admit the impertinence of forcing her unwanted advice on me when I never asked for it. Yet why should she always be telling me what to do? It is quite uncalled for. She is not a relation.'

'You have no relations in London to advise you. If your mother were here it would be different, but she cannot leave your father. My Brunard aunt and cousins are all very amiable but they are not much interested in dress and I've never eaten a well-cooked meal in that house. So I particularly asked Decima to keep an eye on you. Poor girl, I'm afraid she finds it a thankless task when you are always so touchy.'

'I am not touchy!' exclaimed Pamela. 'Well, perhaps I am a little, but at least I am not disloyal.'

'What exactly do you mean by that?' he asked in a chilling voice.

'I call it disloyal of you to discuss me with your mistress.'

'With my *what*?'

They stared at each other, Pamela almost as astonished as Richard. She did not for a moment believe that Decima was his mistress and she did not know what had made her say so. She could see that he was extremely angry. The white line of the scar was rippling on his cheek as though he had a nervous tic. She thought he was going to hit her.

Then he put his hands in his pockets and spoke with a clipped precision.

'I have not got a mistress. I have not been with another woman for over a year. I gave all that up when I married you, which was a good deal more than you deserved, considering how little you've ever tried to please me. But never mind that. I dare say the family reputation has misled you. What I can't and won't stand is to hear you slandering a woman of the most impeccable virtue who is as good as she is beautiful and whose only sin against you has been to try and save you from making a fool of yourself because you are spoilt and ignorant and childish. And if I ever hear that you've spoken a word of scandal about Decima outside this room, I'll take you straight back to Mallowdown and you'll never set foot in London again. Now say you're sorry.'

'No, I won't!' shouted Pamela, rushing from the room and slamming the door behind her.

She ran upstairs in a furious temper which she had to check on entering her bedroom, for her maid Toller was there, smiling and waiting to congratulate her on the success of the dinner party. She had heard every detail in the servants' hall.

Mistress and maid had become fond of each other during the year they had been together, but Toller was not like one of the old servants at home who had known Pamela since she was a child. It was not possible to break down and cry with vexation while she was there. Stifling her feelings, Pamela agreed that the party had gone very well, but now she was tired to death. She allowed Toller to help her undress and prepare for bed.

She felt safe in here from any further lectures from Richard that night. He slept in his own room across the landing. They had not shared a bed since she had begun to feel very ill and uncomfortable early in her pregnancy and he had suggested she might prefer to be alone. He had never accused her of shamming in order to get rid of him. The birth of the twins had vindicated all her claims of feeling much more sickly than anyone—especially Decima—expected.

When they came to London after her recovery she had waited for Richard to move back and assert his rights. When he did nothing it was a relief. She was fond of him now but she did not expect any pleasure from that aspect of marriage. Her mother had warned her that men were made differently—a fact that was remarkably obvious—and that silent co-operation was all a husband could reasonably demand. She supposed Richard would want her to have more children, and indeed she would like a little daughter, but surely she need not go through all that again so soon.

She was disconcerted when Richard walked into the room, without knocking, in his dressing-gown. A new one, she noted absently, with sinuous oriental patterns on the dark Indian silk. He spoke pleasantly to Toller—he was always considerate to servants.

'Her ladyship will have no further need of you this evening.'

'Very good, my lord. Goodnight, my lord. Goodnight, my lady.'

Toller trotted off, knowing on which side her bread was buttered.

Pamela got up from the dressing-table, vulnerable in her thin lawn nightdress, yet able to say in a cool, provocative voice, 'You do not have to be so high-handed because you are in a bad temper.'

Richard ignored this. He said, 'You accused me of having a mistress. I'm afraid you must think I've been neglecting you. This is going to be put right. Get into bed.'

Pamela did not move. She waited to see what he would do next.

He crossed the carpet and took her firmly by the shoulders. She tried to escape from a possessive grip that was unfamiliar and frightening. The more she struggled the harder he held her, tilting her head back so that he could kiss her mouth. Something very odd was happening to Pamela. Always before she had been passive and docile and she had felt nothing beyond the pointless discomfort of what was being done to her. Now that her blood was up and she was ready for a contest of wills, she found that her body was charged with an unknown excitement and—this was the surprising part—the strength and energy that should have enabled her to break away from Richard was acting like a magnet in drawing them irresistibly closer, so that all her instincts told her what she wanted and had never understood before.

He lifted his head, smiling, his eyes very bright.

'It will all go well this time, my darling.'

He picked her up very gently and placed her on the bed. Then he lay down beside her without extinguishing the candles as he had used to in that great room at Mallowdown.

It was the first time they had ever made love visibly, surrounded by a soft golden light. In a sense it was the first time they had ever made love, despite the existence of the twins, asleep in their cradles upstairs. This was entirely different.

CHAPTER SIX

PAMELA was transported with happiness and so too, apparently, was Richard, watching her every movement with that smile at the back of his eyes which suddenly changed him, melting the hardness, the chilly reserve.

'Why was it never like this before?' she asked the following night when they were lying in bed, talking.

'Because you were so dead set against me that I couldn't do anything with you. It was like sleeping with a clothes-horse. Excessively uncomfortable.'

'But I never refused or resisted,' she said in a small, puzzled voice. 'I didn't know how else I was supposed to behave. Richard, had it anything to do with something you said once, about my not liking to look at you, because of the scar? I've always been so ashamed of that.'

'You must not be,' he said quickly, for she was almost in tears. 'It was natural for you to be put off by the sight of such an ugly fellow, and I ought not to have let your father talk me into marrying you so soon, before we got to know each other properly. Last year, when we started so badly, it was mostly my fault. I believe I was as nervous as you were. If we'd been in love already we should have got over that hurdle. As it was, I found myself at a loss. I'd never had anything to do with an innocent young woman.'

'Oh,' said Pamela, who had never thought about this. 'Have you had a great deal to do with—with women who are not so innocent?'

'Yes, I'm afraid I have. But it didn't help.'

He had said when they were quarrelling last night that he had given up all that when they married and she recalled a note of complacency in his voice, as though he had made a heroic sacrifice. This had infuriated her at the time; now she found it rather amusing.

She still did not know why he had chosen to marry her, but at least he had made it plain that he was not in love with Decima, and Richard, drawing her into his arms, made it plain that he did not want to talk any more.

In her new state of confidence and buoyancy she felt quite friendly towards Decima. When they next met she was able to say quite spontaneously that she was afraid she had been cross and stupid on the night of their dinner party, while Decima was saying at the same moment that she had never meant to upset dearest Pamela and what an excellent hostess she had been. So peace was restored and there was no need to feel guilty and uncomfortable.

Richard and Pamela went about a great deal together, riding or driving, dining with friends, going to the theatre and to balls. For it was now April, Lent and Easter were over, and the London Season was in full swing. When Richard was at his club, or attending the House of Lords, Pamela had cosy gossiping sessions with her women friends or went with them on glorious shopping expeditions.

She also spent a great deal of time in the nurseries at the top of the house, cuddling the twins by turns or gazing at them for long silent stretches, making out family likenesses and imaginary signs of intelligence. She longed for the time when they would be old enough to play with.

They were just over three months old and doing well. One morning Roly, the younger twin, had a little rash. Pamela sent for the doctor who had been recommended to them by Lady Brunard. He came and prescribed a bottle of lotion which cleared up the trouble in a few hours.

Two days later, when she returned home from visiting a friend of her mother's, Pamela noted a carriage drawn up outside their door, not a fashionable conveyance but the sort of sober vehicle used by professional men.

'Is there somebody with his lordship?' she asked the footman who let her in.

'Yes, my lady. The doctor called and his lordship has taken him up to the nurseries.'

'The doctor!' exclaimed Pamela.

Not waiting to hear any more, she ran up three flights of stairs and arrived panting on the landing just as Richard came out of the nursery, accompanied by a portly personage she had never seen before.

'What's wrong?' she demanded. 'Which of them is it? Only tell me what's happened.'

'Nothing is wrong,' Richard assured her. 'I'm sorry if you have been alarmed, my dear. Let me present Dr Hillman to you. He has just been telling me what a fine pair of infants we have.'

Pamela took in the portly personage and said, rather accusingly, 'You aren't Dr Jones!'

Dr Hillman agreed that he was not Dr Jones. He sounded rather stuffy about it. It was Dr Jones who had been to see Roly two days ago.

'Then I don't understand why——' began Pamela, but she broke off, receiving a glance from Richard which meant unmistakably, Not now.

Dr Hillman then made a little speech, congratulating her ladyship on her beautiful children, whose excellent health and contented appearance was a credit to her and to her nursemaid. Pamela could hardly listen with civility. As soon as he and Richard started downstairs, she burst into the nursery to see with her own eyes whether her precious babies were safe.

One of them was in his cradle, whimpering in a disgruntled manner, the other was on Nurse's knee having his pilch fastened. Nurse was muttering ominously under her breath.

'What's been going on?' asked Pamela. 'Why was the doctor sent for?'

'Well may you ask, my lady, for I never had any hand in it and no cause to, the little lambs being as merry as crickets, as your ladyship saw when you was up here first thing this morning. And when his lordship walks in with the medical gentleman, all unannounced, you could have knocked me down with a feather. And the place not fit to be seen,' added Nurse, whose domain was, as usual, absolutely spotless and shining with polish. She had two under-nursemaids and a nursery footman at her command.

'Well, I don't understand it.' Pamela picked up the crying baby and looked at his wrist to identify him. 'Poor little Ricky, did the nasty doctor wake you? Give Mama a smile.'

As soon as the babies had been soothed and settled, and Nurse more or less pacified, Pamela went to find Richard. He was in a small room at the back of the hall which he had taken for his study.

He said once more, 'I'm so very sorry, my dearest girl, that you were frightened by the doctor's being here. I had not realised you had gone out and I had no chance of telling you.'

'Telling me what? Did you think there was something wrong with the children? Nurse says they have both been perfectly well, and in any case it is Dr Jones who is looking after them.'

'That's just the point. I know Jones is the Brunards' doctor, and I am sure he would be the right man to call in if you were ill or if I were. But the twins are another matter. When it comes to dealing with young children, Hillman is the first physician in London— far more experienced than Jones. It's as well to be on the safe side.'

'Well, I never thought you'd be such a nervous parent,' said Pamela, staring at the veteran of Waterloo. 'And had anything been missed? What did Hillman say?'

'He said that Jones's diagnosis was perfectly correct.'

'I still don't understand what made you decide to call in Hillman.'

There was a perceptible pause before Richard said, 'Decima recommended him.'

'Decima!'

'Now, my darling, don't fly into a tantrum at the mere mention of Decima. She has young children of her own, unlike Aunt Brunard, so it is only natural she should be better informed about doctors. She thought we should be wise to get a second opinion.'

'I can't imagine how she knew we had consulted Jones.'

Pamela had taken good care not to mention this when they had met the Strangs at Almack's two days before.

'I told her when I called in at Albemarle Street yesterday.'

'How could you?'

'Well, why not? It's wasn't a secret.' Richard seemed genuinely puzzled.

Pamela was still wearing her bonnet. Now she pulled at the strings and dragged it off in an access of frustrated rage. If it hadn't been so pretty she would have stamped on it.

'How could you sneak round to Albemarle Street and confer with Decima behind my back? Telling her, I suppose, that I wasn't taking proper care of your children. I wonder you didn't invite her to come over here and superintend our nurseries herself. You may still have to do so and I dare say Nurse will give warning.'

'I doubt it,' said Richard easily. 'This is the best place she's ever had and she knows it. And I don't need your permission to call in Albemarle Street. As a matter of fact I wanted a word with Hubert.'

'I don't believe you. No one wants a word with Hubert. He is the greatest bore in London.'

'So then I went upstairs to pay my respects to Decima,' continued Richard, disregarding this interruption, 'and when she asked most affectionately about you and the twins, I said we had sent for Dr Jones to see Roly. And she told me in such a case she would have consulted Hillman. That's all there was to it. And the one thing I'm sorry for is that I managed so badly that you were frightened when you came in and heard the doctor was here.'

And that apparently was the only thing he did regret. Pamela had been given an unnecessary scare about her babies and he thought this was the real reason for her waspish remarks.

While she was slowly taking this in, the long-case clock in the corner rang out its deep sweet chime. They were obliged to go and change for dinner. They were going that evening to a ball at a great house on the river; Pamela had been looking forward to it. Now she felt her evening had been spoilt. She no longer thought Richard and Decima were in love, at least not in the ordinary sense of the word, but she thought their mutual reliance, affection, admiration—call it what you would—was stronger than it ought to be between two people who were each married to someone else. It was unflattering, insulting even, how often he discussed matters with Decima that he did not discuss with her.

When they set out two hours later, they were alone in their carriage with a longish drive ahead of them. Richard sat back and stretched his legs. He was in knee-breeches with white silk stockings and buckled shoes, worn only now for grand occasions. He looked impressive, almost handsome. She had his good side next to her, the profile without the scar. As they drove westwards along Piccadilly, he made various remarks about the traffic, the new buildings that were springing up everywhere, the illustrious family whose party they were going to.

Pamela replied with discouraging politeness. At least she thought she was being polite until he asked, 'Are you going to sulk all the evening? Because if so I may as well save my breath.'

'I wasn't sulking.'

She thought it extremely unfair, because he was fourteen years older; he could somehow look down on her from a great height and treat her as though she were a child. It was age rather than sex which gave him this superiority, for Decima had it too. Of course age did make a difference; she was still only eighteen and if she had been brought up to London, unmarried, to enter society in virginal white and speak when she was spoken to, then she would not have expected to be treated as an equal by persons of the consequence of Lord Blaise or Mrs Strang. But she was a married woman and a mother. It was Richard himself who had insisted on marrying her, practically out of the schoolroom, and against her will as it happened. He ought to recognise the fact by trusting and treating her accordingly. She was wondering if she could explain this to him when he spoke again.

'You really have no need to be jealous of Decima. I'm afraid I may have given you a false impression. I know I was angry the other night when you suggested that she was my mistress——'

'I didn't believe that, Richard. I lost my temper.'

'But I think you did believe there was an attachment between us. I promise you it was not so. We've been friends since childhood. You know I was at Harrow with her brother. There has never been an inclination towards anything closer, on either side. Will you try not to let that suspicion worry you any longer?'

'It never has worried me.'

Which was true. During the time she had imagined them as the virtuous victims of a self-denying love, she had not cared very deeply because she had not yet fallen in love with Richard herself, had not ever realised she was heading in that direction. And from their first experience of passionate lovemaking she had been certain instinctively that she was not sharing this side of his life with any other woman.

'I'm very glad to hear it,' he said. 'Though I'm damned if I know, in that case, what you have against poor Decima.'

Pamela pondered and answered honestly, 'I don't like her.'

'Don't like her!' He was amazed and indignant. 'How can you possibly not like her? Considering how charming and sweet-natured and unselfish she is, and how good she has been to you. I never heard such a cold-hearted return for so much kindness. I tell you what's wrong with you, my girl. If it isn't jealousy, then it's envy, which is far worse. Jealous people do deserve compassion if they truly believe themselves justified. Envy has no such excuse. I think it is the only sin which has no mitigating side to it.'

Pamela felt the tears rise in her throat. She choked them back but said nothing. How could she explain her dislike of being patronised and managed and overruled in her own home by a woman who was far more experienced and accomplished and acting from the highest motives? He would simply say that such an ungenerous and grudging spirit was a proof that she was consumed by envy—and perhaps he would be right.

They had reached the end of their journey and stepped out on to a strip of red carpet between an avenue of burning torches.

The house was very large, crowded to the doors, and vibrating with music and voices. Light from the great chandeliers flashed back from shining wall mirrors and from the jewels worn by all the married women.

Pamela was still inclined to be overcome by very grand parties and tonight she was already cast down by Richard's cruel accusation. But the two things worked together. Hurt feelings were more easily hidden while they moved very slowly through the crush and she smiled and bowed like an automaton, repeating a few parrot phrases to those of the other guests she already knew. A great many more knew Richard. There were soldiers here who had not seen him for several years and who came up to shake his hand and greet him with enthusiasm.

'My dear Cressinder—I beg your pardon, Blaise! Delighted to see you again. And you are a married man with a son already... Two, is it? Congratulations, my dear fellow!'

Richard would then present the speaker to Pamela, and watch with complacency the effect of her vivid good looks on his friend. At least, she thought, he is not ashamed of my appearance.

After the success of the pink dress, she had decided to go on with daring colours. Tonight she was wearing peacock taffeta shot with bronze and embroidered all over the skirt with tiny amber beads.

There was so much social conversation that it was a long time before they reached the ballroom. Just inside they met the Strangs. Decima asked after Roly.

'He is fully recovered,' said Pamela before Richard could get a word in, 'and I must thank you, dear Decima, for recommending Dr Hillman.'

She saw Richard's look of approval, while Decima swallowed the tribute like a cat receiving a bowl of cream. Neither of them knew what she was going to say next.

'I only hope,' she continued in her sweetest voice, 'that Hillman will turn out as quickly for Richard or me if ever we need a doctor.'

'But Hillman is concerned with the diseases of childhood,' said Decima. 'Surely you would call in Dr Jones?'

'Dr Jones might not want to come. I expect he has his pride like anyone else. It's odd how discontented people become when they find themselves mistrusted and their territory invaded by meddling outsiders who question their ability and try to do everything differently.'

Decima opened her mouth and shut it again. For once her expression was perfectly blank. Richard promptly asked her to dance with him, ignoring his wife.

'I ought to ask you to dance with me, Pamela,' said Hubert unhappily, 'only I dare say you would not care for it.'

Pamela was taken aback. Did he think she wanted to quarrel with him because she was annoyed with his wife? Or was he unwilling to dance with her because she had dared to criticise Decima? He stood beside her, large and melancholy, his legs, in white silk stockings, much too long and thin. He reminded her of some strange wading bird. But he was not unfriendly, merely apologetic.

'I have never been able to get the hang of these new-fangled quadrilles. I'm afraid I am a severe liability to Decima in a ballroom. Would you mind if we sat and watched?'

'Of course not,' she replied instantly.

They sat against the wall on prim gold chairs and observed the dancers taking their places, four couples in each set. Quadrilles had quite superseded the old country dances in which everyone careered up and down the whole length of a ballroom, weaving in and out and linking arms with everyone else. Quadrilles were more intimate and civilised, friends joining together and performing all the steps within their own set. Pamela could see Richard and Decima talking to each other with great animation. Both were graceful dancers. Richard, though now a civilian, had all the panache of a dashing hussar. Decima looked charming with her dark hair and her silver dress.

But they are not in love, Pamela reminded herself, and however much she enrages me, I must remember that.

'They appear to great advantage, your husband and my wife,' said Hubert Strang. He sighed heavily. 'She deserves a partner with his presence and address. I myself am not well fitted for town life.'

Pamela was sorry for him, and for having called him the greatest bore in London, even though he didn't know it.

'Are you wishing yourself at Bourne House, sir?' she asked sympathetically.

'Yes, I must admit I am. Or better still, in Yorkshire.'

'Yorkshire?'

'I have a property up there which I inherited when my mother died. She was a Thorpe of Herrisdale, the last of an ancient line. I have never lived there myself, but I used to spend long holidays with my grandparents when I was a child, and the place means more to me than Bourne House, which my father purchased forty years ago. Decima tells me I am too romantic and unpractical, but she has no childish memories of Warby. Ladies do not like a very remote situation.'

It was difficult to think of Mr Strang being too romantic, even about a house. He was intensely devoted to his wife, but it was the devotion of a faithful old dog, hardly inspiring. Pamela wished they would both go and live in Yorkshire, but it was not very likely. There was no doubt who made the decisions in that family.

The quadrille was ending. The sets broke up. Hubert stood up as Richard and Decima came towards them. Richard was looking too serious for a ballroom and Pamela felt sure she was going to get a scolding for her impertinence to good, kind Decima. It was more than she could bear.

Looking round hurriedly for a way of escape, she found that the person nearest to her was Lord Charles Everard, whom she had particularly liked ever since he had sat next to her at her famous dinner party.

Catching her eye, he asked in his engaging way, 'Is anything the matter?'

'Would you please talk to me for a moment? There is someone I am trying to avoid.'

'I am at your service, ma'am.' Glancing over her shoulder, he added, 'I hope the person you are trying to avoid is not Richard.'

Pamela felt herself blushing and muttered something about the Strangs.

'Ah, yes, I understand. One's country neighbours are very well *in* the country but the best reason for coming to town is to get away from them. I think the band is going to play a waltz. May I have the honour?'

She was very glad to accept. Lord Charles was a capital waltzer and as they circled the ballroom with the other spinning couples, his arm around her waist, she was able to forget the complications of her life in the sheer pleasure of movement.

When the music died away they were near a door which opened into a garden.

'Shall we go out for a breath of air?'

They stepped on to a terrace overlooking the river. It was a fine May evening with a rising moon. There were lanterns glowing in many of the trees. They walked a little way, then stopped to lean on the balustrade and listen to the rippling sound of the water.

'How beautiful it is here,' she said. 'What is that building on the opposite bank?'

As he began to describe their surroundings, a french window opened immediately behind them and the figure of a woman was illuminated by a roomful of light.

'Emily, come and join us,' exclaimed Lord Charles. 'I'm giving Lady Blaise a geography lesson. She doesn't know the difference between Surrey and Middlesex.'

'Well, why ever should she?' said Emily Everard, coming out on to the terrace. 'I wonder you can be so thoughtless, Charles. Waltzing the poor girl to a standstill and then bringing her out here to catch cold in the night air. I apologise for Charles, my dear. He doesn't know any better. I think you need to be wrapped up.'

She was carrying a Chinese silk shawl over her arm and she proceeded to drape it round Pamela's shoulders. Pamela protested.

'Lady Charles, you must not. I cannot wear your shawl, it is you who will catch cold.'

'No, because I have not been dancing, so I am not overheated. How brilliant the stars are. We hardly see them in London since they invented the gas-light.'

'It seems almost wrong to stay in town at this time of year,' remarked Pamela.

'I often feel the same,' said Emily. 'I miss my home, especially when the roses are out.'

'You and Richard must come and stay with us at Bradwyn,' said her husband. 'Not for a grand house-party; we like to be very informal when we are there. Emily is the perfect hostess—she lets everyone do as they please, copes with amateur theatricals in the drawing-room, impromptu regattas on the lake and never turns a hair when the hunting contingent come home two hours late for dinner and with six unexpected guests.'

Emily gave a small, pleased laugh. 'The secret of living with you, dear Charles, is to remember that nothing can ever be entirely unexpected.'

Pamela sensed the strong current of affection between them. Emily Everard was not as handsome as her husband; in spite of her great elegance her features were rather plain, but Charles's obvious admiration made her glow. It must be delightful to have such a happy marriage.

As she was thinking this, Pamela heard a familiar step on the terrace, one she would recognise anywhere, even with so many people walking about. She turned to see Richard coming towards them. He was clearly visible in the moonlight and there was a grim expression on his strong, war-ravaged face. Then he saw the trio by the balustrade and his mouth relaxed a little.

'I've been looking for you,' he said to Pamela, though she thought she detected a note of accusation.

'I'm sorry,' said Charles, 'I should have brought your wife back to you. We were tempted out here by the fineness of the night.'

'And we have been gazing at the stars and extolling the virtues of country life,' added Emily, 'when all the time we were very pleased to be at this charming party.'

Richard laughed. Pamela was beginning to feel very uncomfortable. For a few brief seconds it had seemed odd that Emily Everard and Richard had both turned up to join them by the river. Then it dawned on her that this was no coincidence. They had come out here deliberately because, in leaving the house with Lord Charles, she had done something improper which might give rise to scandal if it were not quickly scotched.

The Everards, having chatted amiably for a few minutes, moved off together; Pamela had to hurry after Emily so that she could return the shawl. Richard remained by the balustrade. Pamela found she was trembling a little and not from cold.

'Are you angry with me?' she asked. 'Ought I not to have come out here?'

'Perhaps it was not very wise.'

'I'm sorry. I didn't think.' Although she had danced with Charles Everard when she had been feeling annoyed with Richard, by the time they went into the garden she had been simply drawn by the cool evening air. She was not escaping from Richard, avoiding Decima, or hoping for a flirtation with a man who was in love with his own wife. Surely what she had done was not so unheard of? There were plenty of other couples wandering around. What else was the garden here for?

'Am I lost forever?' she asked with an attempt at flippancy. 'Shall I be drummed out of Almack's?'

'I don't think so.' She thought he was smiling now, but he added quite seriously, 'There are people here this evening who have only just met you. It's a pity to give a wrong impression.'

That sounded like a quotation from Decima, but she had enough sense not to say so.

She asked instead, 'Was it wrong of me to waltz with Lord Charles?'

'No, of course not. Why should it be? You've waltzed before at all the balls we've been to.'

'Yes, I know, but I was always being told that waltzing was an invention of the devil. My father would have thought it worse for me to waltz with Lord Charles than to take a walk in the moonlight. Of course he is a complete antiquity, poor Papa.'

'Not so antique as all that,' said Richard. 'I once heard Byron declare that the waltz was immoral.'

'Byron said that? Good heavens, how extraordinary!'

'You must remember that he couldn't waltz himself, poor fellow, on account of his lameness. He was a good cricketer though, when we were at school.'

Richard and many of their friends had known Byron well. It was a matter of regret to Pamela that he had gone into exile in Italy before she arrived in London.

'Do you think he'll ever come home?' she asked.

'I certainly hope so.'

They were leaning on the balustrade. She took a sideways glance at Richard, at the scarred profile which no longer repelled her—how could she ever have been so squeamish and unkind? She now thought he looked rather like a Byronic hero himself; not doomed and damned of course, but there was something contradictory in his character that she had not quite fathomed, something connected with his years of campaigning of course, or more likely with his childhood and that selfish, dissolute father. She was compelled to put another question.

'What was Lady Byron like?'

'An extremely tiresome young woman—she couldn't leave well alone. What a lot of things you want to know this evening.'

It was Lady Byron, Pamela knew, who had made such a fuss over her husband's relations with his half-sister, Mrs Leigh, that the whole of society believed them guilty of incest. Yet it had not been absolutely proved. Suppose Annabella Byron had been jealous of their long-standing affection simply because it excluded her? Was it possible that a foolish exaggeration of her grievances had been the real cause of so much scandal and misery?

Richard suddenly leant over and gave her a light kiss on the cheek.

'Whatever made you do that?' she asked, gratified but rather surprised.

'Kiss my own wife at a ball? Shocking, wasn't it? I thought you looked as though life was such a puzzle to you, dear little Pam. Shall we go indoors and have supper?'

Nothing more was said about those earlier clashes or even about the way she had taunted Decima. The evening was not spoilt after all.

CHAPTER SEVEN

FROM then on Pamela took care not to get drawn into quarrels over Decima. Perhaps Richard took care too, but she was not sure of this. He never again did anything so rash as introducing one of Decima's tame doctors into the house, nor did he actually ask Pamela to agree with him when he remarked how how elegantly Decima entertained and what a good cook she had—by implication, better than their own. But he made such remarks in front of Pamela as often as ever, if not more often, and he was continually visiting in Albemarle Street.

Pamela could not feel she was neglected. He was always a charming companion, and he made love to her with tenderness and passion. All the same she felt a little forlorn. Life was infinitely better than it had been before she had fallen in love and made so many discoveries about her own emotions and desires. She had no right to be dissatisfied, yet she could not help looking back on that blissful time, not quite three weeks, between the night of their first dinner party and what she thought of as the Day of Dr Hillman.

She had been so intensely happy, not a cloud in the sky, thinking that she had become everything to Richard once the barriers were down. And it was not true. However much he loved her, he still did not think much of her abilities, did not think she was equipped to manage his home or bring up his children without another woman's advice, and found that other woman's taste and intelligence very much superior. It was stupid to mind so keenly but she did.

She had one thing to be thankful for. Decima had taken the hint and stopped interfering, contenting herself with a suppressed sigh, a raised eyebrow or a maddeningly gentle, indulgent laugh whenever Pamela did, said, bought or wore anything she disapproved of.

Pamela ground her teeth in secret. She could not confide in any of her women friends, that would be disloyal to Richard, and in any case they too might think she was giving way to the hateful pangs of envy, that most contemptible of vices. Because, as far as she could see, everyone else accepted Decima at her own face value and saw nothing to criticise.

There was one exception: Mary Jane Stevens, Alice Fabian's governess. Pamela had grown friendly with this quiet capable young woman who often brought Alice round to visit her in Half Moon Street. She had begun to call Mary Jane by her Christian name and would have been quite ready to have her own name used in return, but she knew this was out of the question. Under the same rigid convention she could not discuss Mrs Strang with her niece's governess.

One day they came near to comparing notes. Mary Jane and Alice were shown into the drawing-room where Pamela was hurriedly writing a note.

'Sit down, both of you,' she said. 'I shan't keep you waiting long.'

She had promised to take them for a drive in her new carriage.

'Can I go up and see the twins, Lady Blaise?' asked Alice.

'Yes, if you like.'

Alice almost ran out of the room and they could hear her clattering up the stairs. She was so quiet as a rule, it was a pleasure to hear her making such a noise.

'Twins do have a curious fascination,' commented Pamela. 'I am sometimes afraid she is more interested in my babies than she is in her own cousins.'

Mary Jane said thoughtfully, 'Alice is not as fond of her cousins as I could wish. I don't mean that she dislikes them; she is far too good-natured. Or that Mr and Mrs Strang treat her any differently from their own children. But of course she knows she is not their child and she resents not being allowed to live in Devonshire with her father.'

'Are you acquainted with Colonel Fabian?'

'Oh, yes, ma'am. I have known him and Lady Isabella in a distant sort of way since I was fifteen. My father is the vicar of a parish adjoining their own.'

At this point there was only one thing Pamela wanted to ask: What did you think of Lady Isabella? But here again such a topic was impossible. Lady Isabella was an adulteress and no respectable clergyman's daughter could be asked to express an opinion on such a person.

Mary Jane was still talking.

'I was engaged as Alice's governess about six months before Lady Isabella—went away. Mrs Strang came down to Devonshire, and, seeing how things were, she took us all back to Bourne House with her: the colonel, Alice and myself. He had been severely wounded, as I expect you know, and his personal misfortunes brought on a kind of relapse. I am sure Mrs Strang did her best to effect a cure, but people are not all cast in the same mould, even when they belong to one family. After a while Colonel Fabian said he could not stay any longer in his sister's house and insisted on returned to Devonshire.'

'Leaving you and Alice behind?'

'Yes. It was thought the most suitable arrangement. At least Mrs Strang thought so, and Colonel Fabian was in no condition to argue. I dare say she was right and it is not my place to disagree. But that is what Alice resents. That she could not go home and live with her papa.'

Mary Jane's voice was colourless but she undoubtedly thought that Decima had made several wrong decisions. Pamela wondered whether Colonel Fabian had taken to the bottle. Although she knew he had been badly wounded, she could not see how his wife's elopement so long afterwards could have affected his physical condition.

She finished her note and then took Alice and Mary Jane for a drive, ending up with ices at Gunters. They sat outside in the open carriage, as many others were doing, and waiters brought the ices out to them on trays. Alice grew quite pink with excitement, laughing and talking much more than usual. Poor little scrap, thought Pamela, it is a pity she cannot always be so natural.

Reluctantly laying down her spoon, Alice asked, 'Shall we have to keep the ices a secret from Aunt Decima?'

Pamela was taken aback. She glanced at Mary Jane.

'Good gracious, no!' said the governess. 'What can you be thinking of, my dear? Of course we must tell your aunt where we have been. She would not object to Lady Blaise giving you such a treat.'

Privately Pamela thought that was just what Decima might object to.

'Then I suppose it doesn't matter,' said Alice. 'Only she likes to give the treats herself.'

And so she does, thought Pamela, struck by this shaft of wisdom out of the mouth of nine-year-old Alice.

Later, thinking over the events of the morning, she decided that she now knew of three people who were not totally convinced of Decima's perfection, and they were all to some extent in her power, dependent on her goodwill. Alice because she was a child, Mary Jane because she was a paid governess, Colonel George Fabian because he was a sick man whose marriage had failed and he needed his sister's help in bringing up his daughter.

Pamela was thankful to have broken her own dependence. She was no longer obliged to accept treats, either in the form of ornamental jardinières, recommended doctors or hints on fashionable dress. She now had a much stronger reason for her resentment—Decima's extraordinary influence over Richard—but it was the original effect of Decima's interfering, patronising kindness that had first put her back up.

A false, flawed kindness surely, compounded by egotism and self-esteem, easily recognised by those who could not get away from it. Common sense or even instinct had made her more subtle in dealing with others, which was probably why Richard, for instance, failed to see through her.

She met Decima that evening, for the Strangs were in the Blaises' box at the opera to see Gluck's *Orfeo*.

Pamela was entranced by the music and the pathos of the story.

'I wonder,' she said during the interval, 'how many husbands would go down to the underworld to find their wives?'

'And how many would ruin everything by failing to follow their instructions,' said Decima. 'Hubert would be sure to turn round to see if I was coming.'

Hubert looked sheepish.

'Richard wouldn't turn round,' said Pamela. 'He'd take it for granted I was coming.'

They all laughed, Richard included.

Then Decima, turning to Pamela, said, 'It is so good of you to take such an interest in Alice. She has become very much attached to you, as I expect you know, though I hope you won't give her too many ices at Gunters.'

'Not if you don't wish it,' said Pamela, prepared to be prickly. 'Do you consider the ices bad for her health, or her character?'

'Good heavens, neither! I am not such a spoilsport. Only I'm afraid the poor child is at present an innocent victim of her mother's notoriety. Isabella created such a scandal and we should prefer to keep Alice in the background for a few more years, until people have had time to forget. Being seen at Gunters is a little too public; the Islingtons might not like it.'

'I'm sorry,' said Pamela rather stiffly. 'I won't take her there again.'

She thought the prohibition ridiculous, but this time she could not accuse Decima of interfering in something that was not her business.

'Though as to the grandparents not liking it,' she said to Richard when they were back in Half Moon Street, 'considering how badly Lord and Lady Islington must have brought up their daughter, I don't see why they should lay down regulations for their granddaughter. Is she never to see either of her parents again?'

'She'll go to live with her father when she's older. I am sure she is better off at present with the Strangs.'

'What is the matter with George Fabian? Does he drink?'

'Not excessively, as far as I know.'

'He must do something irregular, to prevent him having his daughter at home. Perhaps he chases dairy-maids.'

'Dairy-maids!' repeated Richard in some surprise. 'Why should he?'

'Well, you know what I mean. Unsuitable young women. Only Devonshire sounds so bucolic, one feels it ought to be dairy-maids.'

'I'll chase you if you don't stop talking nonsense and come to bed,' said Richard, catching her by the shoulder and swinging her round into his arms. 'Stand still and kiss me properly, you absurd little vixen.'

Pamela did not mind being his vixen, on account of her nearly red hair. She was also his squirrel, his tawny owl, his dear little Pam. She enjoyed all the love-names but was faintly irritated by the diminutive. Being constantly called little reminded her that she still seemed very young to him, a person to be teased and petted and not taken too seriously. She was not even very small; taller than Decima, anyway.

She was always meaning to say all this, only when they were on the verge of making love she did not want to break the spell, and at other times the moment never seemed quite right.

CHAPTER EIGHT

THE following day Pamela had asked Eliza Savage to come with her to the Royal Academy Exhibition at Somerset House. The Scarlet Hussars, Richard's old regiment, were still stationed at Hounslow, but Major Hector Savage had an appointment at the Horse Guards. Like many cavalry officers, he had a large private income as well as his pay, so he and his wife went about a good deal and knew most of the same people as the Blaises.

While they were having a light luncheon at Half Moon Street, Pamela drew the conversation round to Decima. She had decided to put her new theory to the test.

'Do you like Mrs Strang?' she asked.

Eliza considered. 'Yes, I think so. I am not particularly acquainted with her but I have always found her agreeable. She has pleasing manners and she is not stupid or insipid as so many women are. If she were to walk in at this moment, I should not find her company unwelcome but of course I could not talk as freely in front of her as I do to you, because you and I are friends.'

'So you don't like her,' Pamela pointed out, smiling.

'I don't know her well enough to pass judgement. Clearly you don't like her.'

'No, I don't, but I wonder if you are able to see why.'

95

This had an extraordinary effect. Eliza was lifting her wine glass to drink. She put it down suddenly, spilling a few drops on the table, which she mopped up with her napkin in a fussy gesture that was most unlike her.

Avoiding Pamela's eye, she said, 'I'm sure it isn't true. Appearances are so often misleading. You have never lived in town before, so you don't know how little foundation there is for most gossip. Your real friends know better than to listen to such stuff.'

Pamela was quite at sea. 'I don't know what you mean, Eliza. What is it that my friends don't believe?'

Eliza did look up then, flushed and very much confused. 'Nothing,' she insisted. 'Nothing at all. Forget what I said. I was talking nonsense. I misunderstood you... Could I have another of those delicious macaroons? I don't suppose your cook would part with the recipe?'

Pamela handed her the plate of macaroons, frowning in concentration. After a moment's deep thought, she asked, 'Are people saying that Richard and Decima are in love...? That he is her lover?'

'It's a silly rumour,' declared Eliza. 'Oh, dear, how could I have been so stupid? I thought you must have heard something, when you spoke of a reason for not liking her. I have never believed a word of it and neither has Hector, who knows Richard better than anyone. He says people always told stories about the Cressinder. But Richard is not at all like his father and brother, and even if he were I don't think Mrs Strang is the sort of woman who has lovers. So I do hope I haven't planted any suspicions in your mind, for I'm sure there is no need.'

'No need at all. I know Richard is not her lover.'

'I'm very glad to hear it. But in that case, what are the grounds for your dislike, which you thought I might or might not understand?'

Pamela had been absently drawing lines with her fork through a helping of salmon mousse which she had hardly touched. Pushing aside her plate, she too helped herself to a macaroon and took a large bite.

'Richard is not *in love* with Decima in the ordinary way. I did think he might be until—well, until he made it plain that he was in love with me. When I challenged him, he swore they never had any inclination of that sort towards each other, and I have no doubt he was telling the truth. But she has the most extraordinary influence over him. He admires her excessively, almost as though he were in love, and he is constantly asking her advice, and taking it, what's more.'

'Are you sure that her influence is so great? According to Hector, Richard always makes his own decisions.'

'Oh, yes, about their masculine world: horses and politics and the regiment, that sort of thing. But in the other half of his life, the half he is supposed to share with me, it is Decima who decides what we should do. He defers to her opinion, admires her taste and I am hardly consulted, except as a matter of form. Apparently I am not fit to choose a new carpet or send out invitations for a card party unless Decima is looking over my shoulder, and when it comes to calling in her doctor to look at my children without telling me, I don't care what anyone says—I should not be so mortified if he had half a dozen mistresses and flaunted them all over the town.'

She had not meant to say any of this; she had been bottling it up for weeks and it was only the news that people were gossiping about Richard and Decima that had surprised it out of her. At least Eliza would be an absolutely safe confidante.

She was very much concerned. 'I'm sorry he should have made your life so uncomfortable. I'm sure he cannot have intended to. Have you told him how you feel?'

'Yes, and he said at once I was jealous of her. Later he said I was envious, which is worse.'

'I call that most unreasonable.' Eliza sat silent, thinking, and then said hesitantly, 'I know Richard has no sisters. Mrs Strang is a very old friend; do you think he looks on her as a substitute? Would you find the situation equally mortifying if she were his real sister?'

'I'm not sure. That patronising interference would annoy me just as much, but a brother's affection for his sister is very understandable. I don't think I should resent that, and at least the stupid gossips would not say they were in love.'

Though of course they might do just that, reflected Pamela, remembering the Byrons and Mrs Leigh. Eliza was still in a thoughtful mood.

'When I first met Richard,' she said, 'Hector warned me that his friend Major Cressinder was not at his best with ladies.'

'Good God, what did he mean?'

'That's what I couldn't make out. I half expected one of those rakes who look on all women as their prey and whose civility verges on insolence. That was the reputation of Richard's elder brother. But I could not imagine Hector's being the intimate friend of such a man. So I thought perhaps he was tongue-tied and awkward, caring only for horses, a lout rather than rake. Of course he was neither. He was in every sense a gentleman, well informed, with polished manners and a beautiful dancer—we met at a regimental ball. I asked Hector why he had given me such a description. He said it was difficult to explain. Richard claimed to be out of place in domestic surroundings. He recognised and valued the happiness of married people but did not think he would ever marry himself. At that time there was no likelihood of his succeeding to the title.'

'And when he did,' remarked Pamela with unusual bitterness, 'his idea of settling down was to offer for a girl he'd never met.'

Perhaps after all it was not so difficult to understand why he was able to be a splendid lover and an insensitive husband at the same time.

They drove to Somerset House and she tried to immerse herself in the great exhibition of painting and to forget her own problems. She was studying a small landscape, of Italy perhaps, when she found Lord Charles Everard standing beside her.

'Do you like it?' he asked. 'I've bought it for Emily, for her birthday.'

'It is charming,' said Pamela, thinking that of all the couples she knew Charles and Emily Everard seemed the luckiest and happiest.

They went on looking at pictures for some time, and when Pamela and Eliza left Somerset House, Charles Everard was with them. As they stepped out of the building they passed close to a woman who was coming in. She was a stranger to Pamela, who was intrigued by her beauty. She had brilliant dark eyes and a very white skin, and there was something in her expression which seemed at once mocking and defiant. She looked hard at Pamela and smiled at Lord Charles, who made her a slight bow, though without speaking.

'Who was that?' Pamela asked when they were out of earshot.

Charles Everard glanced at Eliza. 'Did you know her, Mrs Savage?'

'Only by sight; we were never acquainted. It was Lady Isabella Fabian.'

'Just as well. And Lady Blaise, of course, has never seen her before, so you were both spared the embarrassment of having to cut her.'

'Good gracious!' exclaimed Pamela. 'Should we have had to do that? How dreadful for her, poor woman. She is Alice's mother, but I did not know she was in London.'

'Only on a visit, I imagine. I believe she lives in Paris.'

Bel Fabian, divorced and disgraced, was generally spoken of in the past tense, as though she had ceased to exist. She was certainly an exile from the world that Pamela had entered when she married Richard, and it was a shock to realise that she could be physically present in London, walking on the same pavements, breathing the same air as the former friends who had to pretend they did not see her. Virtuous females could have no dealings with a woman who had been divorced. Men, as usual, had more freedom. Charles Everard would probably have spoken to her if he had been alone, but he would not do so while he was squiring Pamela and Eliza.

Normally Pamela would have told Richard about this little encounter when they met at dinner, but that evening she was feeling constrained by the gossip which Eliza had let out by mistake. It did not alter her confidence that Richard was faithful to her within the letter of the law, but it had hurt her pride a good deal, and she did not want to talk to him about other people's marital failures. Besides, any discussion of Bel Fabian was bound to lead to the uncomfortable subject of her sister-in-law. So Pamela kept quiet, feeling she was very unlikely to see the unfortunate outcast again.

Here she was wrong.

Several days later she visited the jewellers just off Bond Street who had taken care of the Cressinder family jewels during the long period when there had been no Lady Blaise to wear them. Several of the heirlooms had been reset for Pamela and one of the diamond bracelets, though very pretty, was so tight on her arm that it was painful to wear.

'It needs to be loosened a little, though I don't see how you are to do it without affecting the design,' admitted Pamela.

Mr Lambardier, the owner of the shop, inspected the bracelet on her wrist, clicked his tongue and said he thought he could get over the difficulty by inserting a different clasp. 'If your ladyship will be so good as to wait a few minutes, I will show you an example of what I have in mind.'

He then disappeared into a workroom at the back, leaving Pamela with nothing to do but overhear a conversation between the only other customer and a subordinate jeweller who were seated in a kind of alcove and partly hidden from her by a screen.

She understood the purpose of the screen when she realised that this was a rather embarrassing transaction, for the lady had come to sell and not to buy.

'Surely you can run to a hundred guineas?' she was saying in a bored voice with a slight drawl. 'The brooch came from you and I know it cost the earth.'

'It was made some time ago, my lady, and I fear this style is no longer much in demand.'

My lady, thought Pamela. I wonder who she is. She did not recognise the voice, and when Mr Lambardier came back she had to listen carefully to what he said about adapting her bracelet, so she did not hear whether or not the woman behind the screen accepted the price she was offered, and she scrupulously avoided looking round when the woman left the shop.

When Pamela herself left the jewellers a few minutes later, her smart town carriage with the coronet on the door was outside waiting for her. She was climbing in when she discovered that there was already someone sitting in one corner, and the beguiling voice spoke to her.

'Do pray forgive me, Lady Blaise. I told your man that you had allowed me to wait for you here. I am so very anxious to speak to you. About Alice.'

Meeting the dark, appealing gaze of Bel Fabian, Pamela was in a quandary. This stranger was the divorced wife of Richard's lifelong friend, a person who had no right whatever to accost her, not even the tenuous claim of old acquaintance. Yet there was a pathetic entreaty in her words and in her glance, and how was it possible to repel her with a cold disdain and turn her out of the carriage while the footman at the open door stood looking on?

Instead she said politely, though without much warmth, 'I shall be glad to drive you wherever you wish to go, Lady Isabella.'

'How very kind of you. To the top of Harley Street, if you please.'

As soon as they were alone and the footman back on the box, they both began to speak.

'I don't know what makes you think you can get into my carriage uninvited——'

'Oh, please don't put on that scolding voice, it reminds me of my sister-in-law.'

Pamela was so horrified by this accusation that she was completely silenced, which gave her unwanted companion a chance to go on talking, most persuasively.

'You are so young and so pretty and you look so kind. I know I ought not to trespass on your good nature and get you into a scrape with Richard perhaps. How is Richard, by the way? Quite a reformed character, I hear, since he came into the title. All I want from you, my dear, is news of my poor little daughter. I know you take an interest in her.

'Do please call me Bel. And you are Pamela, are you not? I never feel like Lady Isabella now. I suppose you know my father will have no more to do with me. But we were speaking of Alice. I hear you took her to Gunters and fed her on ices. I wish I could do that. How does she go on at the Strangs'? I suppose her aunt preaches at her and makes her say her prayers twice as often as anyone else because she is the daughter of a fallen woman?'

To be honest, Pamela had never thought of Decima visiting the sins of the mother upon the daughter. The Strangs were not Evangelical, and if anything the child was being kept back in a state of childish ignorance, not encouraged to brood on sins and situations beyond her understanding. Yet thinking of Alice, so pale and quiet and unnaturally well-behaved, she wondered whether Decima had some subtle way of making the little girl feel guilty and ashamed. She remembered what she herself had endured last year when she had been feeling so ill; a reproving lecture, more in sorrow than in anger, about the feebleness and selfishness of a woman who could not stand up to the trials of pregnancy.

She said cautiously, 'I think Alice misses her home a good deal, but I'm sure her uncle and aunt are kind to her, and she is very much attached to Miss Stevens.'

'Oh, is that girl still with her? Good. She hates me but she won't preach, in spite of her parsonical blood. What makes me angry is that George refuses to let me see my daughter but won't be troubled with her himself. What does he mean by leaving her to the tender mercies of the Lady Patroness?'

'Who?'

'It's my name for Decima; don't you think it suits her?'

In spite of everything, Bel was laughing and Pamela began to laugh too. The very grand leaders of society who organised the weekly balls at Almack's Rooms were known as Lady Patronesses. Decima was not one of these, though no doubt she would have liked to be, and she certainly had two essential qualifications: an extremely high opinion of her own gifts and a strong sense of moral infallibility.

They had now reached the top of Harley Street and Bel tapped on the window, telling the coachman to stop outside a tall brick house on the left.

'I have taken lodgings here for a few weeks,' she announced. 'Discreetly out of the way, don't you think? Come in and pay me a morning call. There is still so much to say.'

A few minutes earlier Pamela would have stiffly refused, but that shared laughter had broken the ice and she could not resist going in for a brief visit to continue the conversation.

The drawing-room was just what she might have expected of furnished lodgings in that part of the town; well appointed but impersonal and a little gloomy. Bel had done a good deal to disperse the gloom by having flowers everywhere in bowls and pots and baskets on all the tables and jostling for space on the mantelpiece. She was obviously very untidy; there were books and gloves and parcels everywhere, stacks of china straight from the warehouse, and an open card-table with last night's cards flung down anyhow and the mother-of-pearl counters heaped together on the green baize.

'The Lady Patroness wouldn't like that,' commented Pamela. 'She told me once that to leave cards lying about after the game was over was a sign of vulgarity.'

'I can just hear her. What a detestable woman she is.'

The new friends sat down to enjoy themselves, as Bel put it, in decimating Decima.

'It's lucky I can find her so amusing,' she said at last. 'It is all the good she has ever done me. In effect she has ruined my life. George would never have divorced me if it hadn't been for Decima.'

Pamela did not know what to say. Although strictly brought up by her old-fashioned and extremely moral parents, since coming to London she had met quite a lot of women who had secret liaisons without ever embarrassing their husbands or anyone else by creating public scandals. The fact that Decima herself could be suspected of being Richard's mistress was enough to demonstrate how these women were regarded; their faults condoned because they were careful and responsible, never allowing their passions to get out of control and shipwreck a whole family's happiness. It was the total selfish abandon of a declared wanton that was thought so shocking. And Pamela had no idea what Bel had actually done.

'George went off to fight in Spain and left me to fight for myself,' she was saying. 'I was very lonely.'

'How old was Alice?' asked Pamela.

'Too young to be a satisfactory companion,' said Bel firmly. 'Dearly as I loved her, I needed someone older, someone I could talk to. I was heedless and imprudent, I did wrong without meaning to. But it was all going to be different when George came home. I resolved to be good, only his sisters told him a lot of stories about me, many of them untrue. All this when he was weak and ill. Can you imagine anyone being so wicked?'

'It was very unkind to you both. So then he divorced you.'

'Not immediately. But everything was spoilt, and besides his temper had been much affected by the pain he had suffered. He grew suspicious, began to spy on me, and I was frightened of him.'

Bel's eyes widened as though she was remembering fear. Her beauty seemed fragile and flowerlike in the dark room with all those other flowers.

'I should not have run away,' she said. 'That was cowardly. I never thought he'd refuse to have me back or to allow me to see Alice. Decima persuaded him into both those decisions and that is why I have been so anxious to meet you, my dear. I am hoping, if it is not too much to ask, that you will plead my cause with George. He seems to have fallen out with his dear sister, and as he does not, apparently, want to have Alice with him at Aldercombe, I think he might weaken and let me have her, if only for a few weeks. Would you put in a good word for me?'

'But I've never met Colonel Fabian,' said Pamela.

Bel seemed astonished and disappointed. 'I thought you must have done; he and Richard having always been such close friends.'

Pamela explained how sickly she had been during her pregnancy. 'And I don't think Colonel Fabian has been in town this year. I don't know whether it's worth your while asking Richard.'

'I shouldn't attempt it. He's completely under that woman's thumb,' said Bel with a candour which made Pamela wince, and showing, incidentally, that she was not completely cut off from the talk of the town.

She asked a great many more questions about Alice, and, when Pamela rose to go, begged her with tears in her eyes to come again.

'If you don't consider it too demeaning.'

Pamela heard herself saying she would be delighted to call in Harley Street, and was only sorry that, as things were, she had better not ask Bel to visit her in return.

Going home in the carriage, she did have some qualms. She knew she would have to keep any meetings with Bel secret from Richard. He was not inclined to be censorious, and if she had struck up an acquaintance with any other divorced woman, she almost felt she might have convinced him that this was the way a charitable Christian ought to behave. But not in the case of Bel Fabian. He was far too prejudiced by the horrible stories he had undoubtedly heard from Decima.

Here Pamela's common sense reminded her that some of these stories were true. Bel had not denied that. But if Decima had kept her mouth shut, Bel would not have been publicly disgraced and the Fabians would have remained a married couple, not ideally happy but no worse off than many other couples whom one met every day.

CHAPTER NINE

HAVING decided to keep her fairly innocent secret, Pamela visited Bel several times during the next fortnight. She was charmed by her, sorry for her, indignant on her behalf. Also, though she would not have admitted this, she was glad of the company of someone who shared her obsessive dislike of Decima.

To start with she felt guilty about deceiving Richard, but she soon hardened her heart. She was paying him out and it was no more than he deserved. His attitude to another woman was making her feel forlorn and look ridiculous. Traditionally she should have got even with him by turning to another man for a light flirtation if nothing worse—and there were several men who would have been only too willing. But Pamela did not want to flirt. Before her marriage she had enjoyed the wayward thrills of playing off one very young man against another. Keeping assignations with Ben in the rectory garden, being taught to waltz by Jack Aplin, eluding her parents' vigilance. Now she cared only for casual, infuriating Richard, who teased her and took her for granted and was not even handsome. This maddened her, and if she could not punish him by playing at love with someone else, the next best thing was to cultivate a friendship he knew nothing about and would certainly disapprove of.

She did not say any of this in Harley Street, but Bel was perceptive about other women, like many of her kind.

'You ought to teach Richard a lesson,' she said once. 'What a fool he is to go running after Decima. He'll never climb into her bed.'

'I know that. And he doesn't expect to—I know that too,' said Pamela firmly.

'She's one of those who makes a virtue out of a disadvantage. She was born with ice in her veins. Why do you suppose she married Hubert?'

'I've often wondered. I know he is very rich but she is not worldly.'

'She chose him because he will do everything she wants and make few demands. She may be generous with her time and energy when meddling with other people's lives. Where affection is concerned, she is a taker not a giver.'

'She is very fond of Hubie and Dessy,' said Pamela doubtfully.

'Oh, yes—fond. I dare say she may even be fond of my poor little Alice. She does not love those children, any more than she loves her husband or yours. She is incapable of loving. I cannot bear to think of my daughter growing up in that household of lukewarm propriety, thinking that none of us cares for her.'

Bel was very anxious to see Alice and still hoped this might somehow be managed through Pamela, who had now been told a good deal about the Fabians' unhappy marriage.

Bel had been visited in Devonshire by her former lover. She admitted that he had been her lover while George was in Spain, but he had come to Aldercombe simply as an old and dear friend. George would not believe this, and he had behaved with such brutality that she had run away. Yes, it was true that she had gone to London with her friend, but he was acting only out of chivalry and it was not an elopement. They had parted soon afterwards; surely that proved their innocence? The House of Lords had not thought so. Horrible old men, they were all hypocrites and her father was the worst of the lot. Condemned by the passing of the private Bill which had granted her husband a divorce, she had gone to live abroad, grieving for the loss of her daughter but believing that George would take good care of her. It was only when she had come back to England that she had discovered that Alice was now separated from both her parents and was being brought up by the hated Decima.

'If you could arrange for me to see her just once, my dear Pam, before I return to France, then I could explain that I never meant to desert her, to disappear without even saying goodbye. She must think me utterly heartless.'

'I wonder if a single meeting might not do more harm than good,' said Pamela doubtfully, 'if it were to stir up old memories and make her unhappy.'

Bel did not agree. 'If you were in her place, wouldn't you prefer to feel sad for an hour or so in order to learn that your mother still loved you and thought of you continually? Children are very resilient. And there is one more consideration. If Alice expresses a wish to see me when she is older, I don't believe George will stand in her way. He may not suggest or encourage a meeting, but if she asks he won't refuse. Only she will have to do the asking, and she never will unless I can see her before she quite forgets me, and sow the seeds in her mind.'

Pamela went home in a state of confusion. She sympathised with Bel and entered into all her feelings. She knew how dreadfully she would suffer herself if she were ever cut off from the twins, but she did not want to take part in a scheme which might seriously disturb Alice. How it would affect Decima or Richard or the unknown Colonel Fabian, if they found out, she hardly considered.

She sent a note to Miss Stevens asking her to bring Alice round to Half Moon Street next day. As it was raining hard, they stayed indoors. Pamela challenged Alice to a game of spillikins. A box of tiny ivory shafts and spindles was tipped on to the table in a criss-cross heap like a badly made bird's nest and each player, armed with an ivory hook, took turns in trying to extract one piece from the entanglement without allowing any of the others to move. The player who extracted most pieces won the game.

Alice was an expert. She flipped out the tiny stems of ivory and soon had twice as many as Pamela, who was preoccupied, wondering how she was to introduce the awkward subject of the child's runaway mother.

Then Alice herself provided a heaven-sent opportunity.

'I used to play spillikins with my mama when I was little,' she remarked, without any apparent emotion.

'Did you, my love?' Pamela glanced round. She had offered Mary Jane Stevens a book of Oriental scenes to look at, and the governess was studying these, paying no attention to the spillikin players. This was a perfect chance to test Alice's feelings.

'How well do you remember your mama, Alice?'

'I haven't seen her for ages and ages.' Alice frowned. 'I do wish she'd come back and then we could go and live with Papa at Aldercombe and everything would be nice again.'

The words wrenched at Pamela's heart. That solution was not very likely—though stranger things had happened and George Fabian had forgiven his errant wife once.

She said, 'Your mama is very pretty, isn't she?'

'She is the most beautiful person in the world,' said Alice with conviction.

After that Pamela told Bel she would help to arrange a meeting.

She would invite Alice out on a particular morning. Decima never made any objection to these outings provided they did not include Gunters. On the drive to Harley Street she would explain who it was they were going to visit, and if Alice showed any sign of being frightened or reluctant or distressed the whole plan would be cancelled. She laid down this condition and Bel had to accept it, which she did with a fairly good grace, though murmuring that the child's own mother knew what was best for her.

If Bel had been staying longer in England, Pamela would have been more apprehensive, thinking that she might demand further secret meetings with her daughter, but she was on the point of returning to Paris. Her passage had been booked on the packet.

On the appointed morning everything went smoothly and Pamela had only one minor problem to deal with. Somehow she had to get rid of Mary Jane to prevent her coming on this expedition. She was not at all sure how long Alice's secret visit to her mother would remain a secret once it was over. She knew that Alice was good at keeping things from Decima, but one could not encourage the child to be deceitful and she was only nine. If the story came out, with disagreeable repercussions, that was a risk Pamela herself was ready to take, but she could not involve a young woman like Mary Jane Stevens with her living to earn. So she concocted another small plot.

'My dear Mary Jane,' she said, when the governess and her charge arrived in Half Moon Street, 'I wonder if you would mind running an errand for me while I take Alice for an airing?'

'I should be very glad to, Lady Blaise. What is it you want me to do?'

'To go to Hatchard's, if you please, and order a book about the Trojan War which they are to dispatch to my father in Bath. All the particulars are written down here except the title, which I have stupidly forgotten, but it is a new book and I am sure you will find it quite easily. In fact, you are the only person I can rely on to carry out this commission for me without getting into a muddle, so I shall be most grateful.'

Pamela was rather proud of her own ingenuity. Everything she had said was true, except that she had not forgotten the name of the book. By pretending to do so, she had made it seem reasonable to ask an educated girl like Mary Jane to go to the bookshop for her, instead of sending a servant with a note.

Mary Jane, quite unsuspecting, was only too glad to walk along Piccadilly and spend a happy morning browsing in Hatchard's while Pamela and Alice drove off in the carriage.

While they were driving up Park Lane, Pamela informed Alice in a matter-of-fact voice that her mother was in England and they were on their way to see her now.

'Provided that is what you would like. We need not go if you don't wish to.'

'Is Papa there too? Will they take me back to Aldercombe?'

'I'm afraid not,' said Pamela regretfully, thinking that the little girl probably missed her old home as much as she missed her parents. She remembered how she herself had longed to be back at Crewse when had she first gone to Mallowdown.

'Your mama lives in France now. She's only over here on a visit. Are you sure you want to see her?'

'Yes, please, Lady Blaise.'

Alice was, as usual, extremely self-possessed. There was no sign of nervous emotion, though she did sit forward as though urging the carriage to go faster and her pale little face had grown quite pink.

When they reached the house in Harley Street, the door was opened, not by a servant, but by a gushing woman of about thirty, elaborately dressed in a style that was a little too young for her.

'May I introduce myself to your ladyship?' she simpered. 'My name is Selina Parkins, and I have been deputed to take care of you while this dear child is with her mama.'

Pamela had not really thought out how the reunion was to take place but she did see that Bel would prefer to have Alice to herself.

She said, 'Shall you mind going upstairs with this lady?'

Alice simply said, 'I want to see my mama.'

She accompanied Miss Parkins without any sign of shyness and Pamela was left alone in a rather depressing dining-room at the back of the house. Not for long, however. Miss Parkins reappeared, gushing and smiling.

'Such an affecting scene—it was a privilege to be a witness, though of course I came away immediately. One would not wish to intrude. And I fancy they will be some little while. Won't your ladyship take a chair?'

Pamela sat down and so did Miss Parkins, who clearly felt it her duty to provide sprightly conversation. Pamela found her irritating but responded politely. She assumed that Miss Parkins either lived or lodged in the house and that this was her dining-room. It soon turned out she was mistaken.

'Good gracious, no, ma'am! I am simply here at Lady Bel's request. She has been so kind to me and any little thing that I can do is a small repayment.'

Pamela wondered what sort of kindness Bel had shown to this vulgar woman. Was it the condescension of an earl's daughter who allowed herself to be toadied by a person she would never have mixed with before her divorce? Perhaps that was an unworthy thought. Still, it did seem odd that Bel should have invited the woman here on the day she was expecting Alice.

It was tedious waiting. Already bored, Pamela began to feel uneasy without quite knowing why. There was nothing surprising in Bel's wanting to keep her daughter to herself for as long as possible.

All the same she kept looking at the clock, and at the end of half an hour suggested that she might now go up to the drawing-room.

Miss Parkins jumped visibly. 'Oh, I don't think, my lady—if you will forgive me—I don't think they will be quite ready. They are preparing a surprise, you know. I was on no account to let you go up too soon.'

Pamela wondered what the surprise was going to be. Had Bel gone out and bought her daughter an expensive present, a new dress perhaps, which Alice was changing into, and which would have to be explained in Albemarle Street as coming from Pamela? This would lead to an awkwardness with Decima, she thought gloomily.

After a further ten minutes she said to Miss Parkins, 'Would you be good enough to go upstairs and remind Lady Isabella that time is passing? We cannot stay too long.'

Miss Parkins gave her an odd look. Then she jumped up and ran out of the room without a word.

The sound came back of her heavy tread on the stairs and after that nothing at all.

Pamela walked up and down the dining-room in an acute state of fidgets. This was ridiculous. Presently she too went out into the hall and climbed the stairs. Bel occupied the only two rooms on the first floor, a large drawing-room and a bedroom behind it. No voices or movements came from either, and that was strange because both doors were open.

When Pamela looked inside she got the shock of her life. All Bel's paraphernalia of extravagant possessions, purchases and ornaments had vanished. The drawers in the bedroom were open and empty, some drooping flowers remained, and there was crumpled paper everywhere, the aftermath of packing.

She stood there, stunned into stupidity. Bel had gone, that was clear, but what had happened to Alice? Had she been abducted by Miss Parkins and her cronies, like somebody in a Gothic novel? Pamela shook herself. Gothic novels did not happen in Harley

Street. She ran downstairs, to confront Miss Parkins who was standing in the hall with a letter in her hand.

'Where are they? What's happened?'

'Dear Lady Blaise, there is no need to distress yourself. I was to give you this letter with Lady Bel's compliments.'

Pamela tore open the letter and read it with fury and disbelief.

> My Dearest Pam,
>
> When you read this I shall be on my way to France with my dear little Alice. Since her father does not wish to give her a home and I do, this seems the happiest solution. You may rest assured that I am not carrying her off against her will—indeed that would not be possible in London and in broad daylight. When you bring her to me this morning I shall ask her if she would like to come and live with me, and, if she says yes, we shall be on our way before Selina Parkins gives you this letter.
>
> I know you will forgive me for deceiving you a little, for you too are a mother and will understand what I have suffered. A thousand thanks for your assistance.
>
> I hope we shall meet again before long, in France perhaps, where people are not so stuffy. Tell Richard he must bring you to Paris soon.
>
> Yours, et cetera,
> Bel.

Pamela felt sick. Everything seemed to be spinning round her and she could hardly think straight. But she had got to keep her head at all costs. She turned on Miss Parkins.

'How were they travelling and where were they making for? Which port?'

The silly woman fawned and fluttered. 'I fear I cannot give you any details, my lady.'

'Then it will be all the worse for you. You have conspired to abduct Colonel Fabian's daughter, and if her mother takes her out of the country you will still be here and you will be put in prison.'

Miss Parkins stepped back with a gasp of fright. 'But I have done nothing—nothing at all!'

'Then tell me how and where they went and we may be able to stop them.'

After gaping at her for a moment, Miss Parkins saw the sense in this.

'They went by the back stairs,' she wailed. 'Out by the area door and up the kitchen steps. There was a carriage waiting for them. That's all I know, my lady. Indeed it is.'

Pamela remember an anonymous hired carriage that had been standing outside when she and Alice arrived.

'They wouldn't go all the way to Dover in a hackney. She had a rendezvous arranged with a post-chaise, hadn't she? You had better tell me where.'

'Of course—how foolish of me—there must have been a post-chaise ordered, but indeed I don't know where. The gentleman arranged it all.'

'What gentleman?'

Miss Parkins did not know what gentleman. She had passed him once on the stairs and he was very handsome, but she had never heard his name. Now thoroughly disillusioned, Pamela reflected that there was bound to be a gentleman involved in any adventure of Bel's. Was she eloping yet again? It seemed incredible, but there was no time to waste.

She ran out into Harley Street, abandoning Miss Parkins who was on the verge of hysterics. Her own carriage was there and the hackney, of course, had gone. She wondered for a second whether to question her coachman, but decided that this would be pointless. That wretched child must have got into the hackney with her mother quite willingly. The hired driver would have had his instructions and the whole conveyance would have disappeared at the end of the street.

So she simply said, 'Please drive me home as quickly as you can. I want to catch his lordship before he goes out.'

She had decided that the only thing she could do was to tell Richard everything. She would have to admit how deceitful she had been, and what a fool, letting herself be taken in by Bel's repertoire of charm and pathos. He would be understandably angry, but that couldn't be helped. She knew how fatal it would be for Alice to be carried off to France. Not because Colonel Fabian had rights over his daughter and Bel had none—she still thought that monstrously unjust— but she had enough sense to know that Bel, exiled from respectable society, had now put herself on the wrong side of the law. A truly loving mother would have recognised that she was not in a position to give her daughter a good, stable home. The French might not be as stuffy as the English, thought Pamela, riled by the impudence of Bel's letter, but she believed that they held strict notions about the upbringing of young girls and would not allow their own children to make friends with the daughter of a woman as notorious as Bel.

The town carriage went jingling down Park Lane at an unseemly pace. The two men on the box were enjoying the treat of carrying out such unusual orders and laughing at the indignant faces of everyone they overtook.

As they swung out of Piccadilly into Half Moon Street, they nearly ran into their employer, who was driving his curricle, and halted very sharply indeed.

Pamela could hear Richard using what she thought of as his regimental voice and some decidedly regimental language. She hung out of the window. 'Richard—thank goodness I've caught you! Don't drive off. I must speak to you.'

'Good God, Pam, what's the matter?'

He got down from his curricle, handing the reins to the groom who was perched up at the back.

'Has there been an accident?' he asked, opening the carriage door. 'You're as white as a ghost.'

'Not here,' she whispered. 'In the house.'

They went indoors and through to the little study.

'Now you can tell me,' he said.

CHAPTER TEN

PAMELA hardly knew how to begin. Richard was so concerned for her, so totally unprepared for what she had done.

'Did Parker frighten you?' he asked. 'He was driving like a lunatic.'

'No, no. I told him to go fast—I knew you would be starting for Chiswick. Richard, the most dreadful thing—I don't know what we can do. Bel Fabian is taking Alice to France.'

'Taking Alice to France! Nonsense, she can't be. What makes you think so? You've never set eyes on Bel as far as I know.'

'Yes, I have. I saw her at Somerset House and then at the jewellers. I visited her at her lodging in Harley Street. This morning I took Alice to see her and they slipped off without my knowing. It's all my fault,' concluded Pamela miserably.

He stared at her, his face hardening into that inscrutable look she remembered from their first meetings. She now knew it was the mask he put on when he wanted to hide what he was thinking.

She dreaded his next words, but he only asked, 'How do you know they were going to France?'

'She left me this letter.'

She handed him the screwed-up sheet of paper, and, when he had read it, added the scraps of information she had bullied out of Miss Parkins.

'Dover,' he said, frowning. 'Thank heaven you had the sense to find that out. I can go straight after them in the curricle. That's a bit of luck too. I won't waste time going to see the Strangs, though I suppose I'd better scribble a note to Decima.'

Pamela hoped he was not going to ask her to deliver the note. She did not at all want to meet Decima and thought of a cowardly way of putting off the evil hour.

'Can I come with you, Richard?'

'To Dover? Whatever for?'

'For the sake of Alice. It would be awkward for you to take her away from her mother.'

'That's true. I need a woman with me.'

The most suitable woman would be either Decima or Mary Jane Stevens, but they were not immediately available and would require lengthy explanations.

'Very well,' he said. 'I suppose you had better come. You'll need a coat and something more sensible on your head than that rosebush. And don't keep me waiting.'

Pamela hurried to collect a driving-cloak for herself and a wrap for Alice. She put on a small, close-fitting bonnet with a veil to keep off the dust, more suitable for an open carriage than the delicious hat Richard had called a rosebush. When she came downstairs again he was already out on the pavement. He could not have spent much time on his note to Decima. She wondered what he had said.

He looked her over dispassionately, lifted her on to the high seat of the curricle and got up beside her before speaking to his man who was holding the horses.

'Get aboard, Primrose. We're on our way to Dover.'

'Very good, Colonel.'

John Primrose had been Richard's groom in the Army. He had followed his employer into civilian life but still insisted on using his military rank instead of his title, to the disgust of some of the other servants. He had a face like that of a wise monkey which did not match his floral surname. He hopped up at the back of the curricle and they bounded away.

For some minutes no one spoke. Richard was too busy driving, working his way through the traffic and seizing every opportunity to get ahead.

Pamela was trying to make some sense out of the disagreeable happenings of the morning and feeling humiliated by her own stupidity.

She knew very well that she should never have taken Alice to see her mother. During those previous conversations in Harley Street, Bel had pleaded her own cause with great skill, but several careless remarks had shown her to be selfish and unscrupulous and not at all sorry about the love-affair which had broken up her marriage. How had she persuaded Alice to go with her, apparently without a second thought? Had she deceived the child too, with promises of some surprise which was not actually on the premises? A pony or a dog, perhaps, that Alice was to have for her very own. It was the sort of inducement that a child would always believe.

They were crossing Westminster Bridge when Richard asked, 'How long were you in that house before you discovered they'd gone?'

'About forty minutes,' said Pamela wretchedly. 'I could kick myself for being so simple.'

'Well, you're not the first to be taken in. She can be very plausible, though her victims are usually male.'

'Are we going to overtake them?'

'Oh, yes,' he said with confidence. 'We have several advantages. They cannot be more than half an hour ahead of us, allowing for the time Bel must have spent in persuading Alice to go with her. They will not have walked straight out of the house together directly they met and she will not be expecting an immediate pursuit. She had a post-chaise waiting somewhere. She does not know that you were able to transfer into the curricle with hardly any delay. Best of all, we can go faster than they can.'

Pamela puzzled over this. 'Surely they'll have four horses. We have only two.'

He glanced down at her with something like amusement. 'My dear mathematician, do you suppose four horses harnessed together are able to go four times as fast?'

Pamela realised that this was just what she had been supposing and of course it was nonsense. She felt sillier than ever.

'A loaded travelling chariot needs a strong team to keep up an average pace,' he said. 'My fellows here make nothing of this little cockle-shell and it is much easier for us to manoeuvre in and out of traffic.'

He demonstrated this by overtaking a slow timber-wagon and slipping through the gap between a gentleman's carriage and a smart little gig coming the other way.

Still he had said nothing to Pamela about the idiotic behaviour which had sent them off on this wild-goose chase. He would not do so, she decided, while Primrose was listening. Some men regarded their servants as pieces of furniture or deaf mutes. That was not Richard's way, and he regarded Primrose, the old soldier, almost as a member of the family.

He was driving skilfully and rather too fast. Pamela, who was not usually nervous, braced her feet against the curved dashboard of the curricle and surreptitiously gripped the edge of her seat as they swung round corners or jolted over rough patches in the road. Houses, churches and villages flew past them and were left behind, divided by fields from the next clump of buildings and people. She had never been on the Dover Road before and had no idea what any of the places were called.

Presently Richard spoke to Primrose. 'The chaise we're after—I don't know where it was hired so there's no guessing where they'll change horses. We'll have to start enquiring at the posting houses.'

'Yes, sir. We're coming up to the Hare and Hounds, just ahead on the left. Who am I to ask for, sir?'

'Better if I do the asking. You look after her ladyship and the horses.'

They stopped outside a busy red brick inn where there were constant comings and goings. Richard went inside. He was soon out in the yard again, looking hopeful.

'We're in luck,' he said, getting back into the curricle. 'They did change horses here and remained about twenty minutes in a private room, I can't think why. *I* shouldn't have wasted so much time while there was any risk of a pursuit.'

Pamela remember something. 'Mary Jane told me once that Alice is not a good traveller.'

'Ah,' said Richard. 'I don't suppose Bel and her *cher ami* bargained for that. We shall be up with them any time now.'

Pamela wondered whether he had any idea who Bel's companion was likely to be and whether it would be improper for her to ask him in front of Primrose. Surely not. Primrose himself was going to have a good look at them. It was all going to be hideously awkward, and the worst part of it would be poor little Alice's disappointment at being dragged away from her mother after their brief reunion.

'There's a post-chaise standing on the verge, Colonel,' announced Primrose, gazing down the dusty road towards a stationary yellow carriage with several people moving around it on the grass: a man, two women and a smaller figure wearing the bright blue gingham dress that Alice had on when she and Pamela had set off for Harley Street.

They were all too engrossed in the little girl to notice the approaching curricle, until Richard drew up immediately behind the post-chaise, flung the reins to Primrose, jumped down and strode toward them, leaving Pamela to get out of the curricle by herself, which was not at all easy in a tight skirt.

As she hurried towards them, she heard Bel's clear, mocking voice exclaim, 'Whatever brings you here, my dear Blaise?'

'I've come to save you from making a fool of yourself. And as for your fellow conspirator in this ramshackle business... Oh, good God! I might have guessed!'

Pamela did not at once find out what it was Richard might have guessed, because she was almost bowled over by Alice, who ran towards her, arms outstretched.

'Oh, Lady Blaise, I'm so glad you've come! I don't want to go to France. I want to go to Devonshire, to my papa!'

'There, my love, you shan't go to France,' said Pamela, hugging her with an immense feeling of relief because she was going to escape the worst consequence of her folly. Apparently Alice was not going to be heartbroken because she could not go to Paris with her mother.

She heard three voices arguing: Richard's, Bel's and another that was surprisingly familiar. Glancing up, she found herself staring straight at Charles Everard.

'Oh!' she said in such astonishment that they all stopped talking and looked at her.

'Did you have to call out the cavalry?' demanded Bel. 'I thought better of you, Pam. I did indeed. And as for you, Richard, I never thought you'd turn into such a moralist. Quite a change from the old days. It must be the influence of Decima.'

Pamela hardly heard her. She was gazing dumbly at Lord Charles. Up to that moment he had seemed as unabashed as his mistress. Now he was decidedly uncomfortable.

He bowed uncertainly, and, catching Pamela's eye, looked away.

Richard said, 'Take Alice and get into the curricle, Pamela.'

She realised he was being protective so did not resent his rather arbitrary manner. She hesitated all the same.

'Should not Alice say goodbye to her mother?'

'Goodbye, Mama,' said Alice hastily, still clutching Pamela's hand.

'I suppose I shall have to let her go,' said Bel. 'Since you're too craven to protect us, Charles. If you had any pride you'd be calling Richard out.'

'No, I shouldn't,' said Everard firmly. 'I haven't a leg to stand on and he knows it. I told you we ought not to take Alice with us, only you must have your own way.'

'I'm not getting it now,' said Bel. Tears welled into her eyes as if by magic and stayed there unshed, adding to their brilliance. She was wearing a sky-blue habit and a tall hat like a man's, and managed to look beautiful, gallant and pathetic at the same time as she stooped to give Alice a light kiss.

'Goodbye, my pet. I'm sorry you aren't coming with us but I dare say it's all for the best. You don't care for long journeys and you aren't used to French food. You can come and see me when you're a little older.'

'Yes, Mama,' whispered Alice obediently.

As Pamela led her away, they were pursued by the fourth member of the party, Bel's French maid, who wanted to offer milady a vinaigrette which she was likely to need since *mademoiselle* suffered so much from the movement of the carriage.

As Primrose was lifting Alice into the curricle, Pamela overheard a low-voiced conversation between Richard and Charles Everard, who were standing in the shadow of the post-chaise. Lord Charles was apparently apologising; at first she was not sure for what. He had committed so many misdemeanours—eloping with Bel, helping her to abduct Alice, abandoning the charming wife who adored him. But it was a different breach of the code which concerned him at present.

'I am afraid Lady Blaise has been placed in a very embarrassing situation,' he said. 'I do sincerely regret it. Will you please tell her so?'

'Never mind your mutual embarrassment. What I want to know is, was it you who introduced her to Bel?'

'Good God, no. I may be a black sheep, but I'm not as murky as that.' Everard sounded shocked. He added with unusual diffidence, 'I hope this business isn't going to put an end to our friendship, Richard?'

'Certainly not. If Bel wanted to carry off her daughter, I don't suppose you were given any choice in the matter. As for the rest, I'm not keeper of your morals, am I? *Au revoir*, my dear fellow, and *bon voyage*. Enjoy yourself among the Frogs.'

Richard got back into the curricle and turned dexterously in a gateway most drivers would have considered too narrow. They were now too overcrowded for comfort, even though Alice was so small, and they stopped at the first posting inn they came to on the London-bound side of the road, where Richard asked if there was a chaise available.

They were in luck. Primrose was left behind to bring the curricle back next day when the horses were rested. Pamela, Richard and Alice stepped into a sedate closed carriage and began their return journey.

Alice was quite prepared to talk about her adventure.

'I never wanted to go to France,' she said earnestly. 'I thought we were going back to Aldercombe, to live with Papa.'

'Is that what your mother told you?' Richard asked.

'Yes, Lord Blaise. At least,' the little girl frowned, striving to be exact, 'it's what I thought she meant. She asked if I should like to come and live with her, and when I said, "Do you mean at home with Papa like we used to be?" she said, "Is that what you would like?" I said, "Yes", and she said, "We'll see what can be arranged," in a smiling sort of way, like people do when you want a particular present for your birthday, and you know that means they are going to get it for you.'

So that's how she lured Alice out of Harley Street, thought Pamela in disgust. What a mean trick to play on a child.

'She said we must go at once because there was a post-chaise waiting for us,' Alice continued. 'And she was leaving a letter for you, Lady Blaise, so you wouldn't worry. We went in a hackney to Lord Charles Everard's house. The post-chaise was there already, and she put me inside to wait for her while she went into the house. When she came out again Lord Charles was with her and I think they'd been having an argument.'

'Were you not surprised to see him?'

'Not at first because I thought he was going to escort us into Devonshire. Mama laughed and said he was our courier and she hoped he wouldn't go on being cross.'

So the journey had begun, Alice still believing they were heading for the West Country. She knew so little of the geography of London that she had not realised they were going in the wrong direction. They had been driving very fast and she had soon begun to feel, not sick precisely, but queasy and uncomfortable. The fear of disgracing herself had filled her mind, so she had paid little attention to the scenery outside the carriage or what her companions were saying to each other. They had stopped a couple of times on the road to give her a breath of fresh air, but it hadn't been until they changed horses, and entered the posting house to take light refreshment, that she had heard a mention of Dover and something about the French packet.

Then she had begun to suspect that she had been duped. She had asked for reassurance, and Bel had gone on pretending they that were on their way to Devonshire, but Lord Charles had put an end to this.

'He said she mustn't tell such stories and he was taking us to France. I didn't know what to do. It wasn't my fault.'

'Did you try to persuade them to take you back to London?' Richard enquired gently.

She had done her best but without success. Though capable of hiding her feelings, she was not a rebel. Life with Decima had taught her to do what she was told.

'Mama said I mustn't be silly. She said we should have a beautiful appartment in Paris and she would give me a French doll with lots of different dresses to put on and off. As though I was a baby still, to be playing with dolls! And I hate living in a town. I want to go back to Aldercombe. To Papa,' concluded Alice, bursting into tears.

Pamela held her close and tried to comfort her.

The day had clouded over, and it was beginning to rain. Richard and Pamela sat silent, with Alice between them. Unable to talk freely in front of her, they did not talk at all.

In spite of Bel's perfidy and the misery of poor little Alice, Pamela found herself thinking chiefly of Charles Everard. Her disillusion with Bel was nothing to her disillusion with him. She had thought the Everards an ideally happy couple, had envied Emily her perfect marriage and her romantically devoted husband. Yes, envy was the word, devoid of its horrid associations, because she had not felt an atom of bitterness or spite, only a wistful longing to believe that Richard admired and idolised her as much as that. And now it turned out that this model husband was eloping to France with Bel Fabian.

Presently Alice dropped off to sleep.

'Best thing she could do,' said Richard, speaking softly so as not to wake her. 'Thank God she did not want to go with her mother. All's well that ends well.'

'Except for poor Lady Charles. How could he desert her to run off with Bel? I had not thought it possible.'

'He hasn't deserted her,' said Richard calmly. 'Emily has gone to visit her invalid sister in Wales, and Charles will be back in England before she returns. He and Bel weren't eloping together, they were simply indulging in the kind of adventure for which they are both equally notorious.'

Pamela felt her mind reeling under another shock. 'You mean he's done it before? Does Emily know?'

'Of course she knows. She always forgives him, which is very sensible of her. She can't change his nature, and in any case she must be aware that he sets a far higher value on her and on their marriage than he does on any of his transient passions.'

Pamela remembered waltzing with Charles at the house by the river. When they had strolled out into the moonlight, Emily and Richard had both come after them. Had they suspected that Charles was intent on a little philandering? Enily had been so friendly and kind to her. She was going to ask Richard about this when Alice woke up and it was not possible to say any more.

They were driving at a snail's pace because if they went slowly enough Alice did not feel sick. It was after four when they again crossed Westminster Bridge. Alice became nervous.

'Do you think Aunt Decima will be very angry with me?'

'No,' said Richard instantly. 'I shall explain what happened and she will know that none of it was your fault.'

She'll know it was my fault, thought Pamela.

Richard said to her, 'We will drop you off at home before going to Albemarle Street.'

He wanted to avoid any recriminations in front of Alice. So Pamela was set down in Half Moon Street, and went indoors feeling cold, tired and apprehensive. She knew that the explanation could not be put off much longer. When she had first told him she had taken Alice to see Bel, there had been no time to waste in outrage and disapproval, and from then on they had not been alone for a single second. But now they would be and she was not looking forward to it.

Richard was gone more than an hour and when he returned from the Strangs Pamela was sitting in the drawing-room in a state of inertia, her self-confidence ebbing.

'Thank God that's over,' he said, carefully shutting the door and coming to stand in front of the empty fireplace.

'Was she—was it very difficult? I hope she did not lay any blame on Alice,' said Pamela, for this really was the aspect which worried her most.

'She was perfectly good-tempered and reasonable, as she always is, treating the matter as lightly as possible so long as Alice was in the room. Afterwards, when we were alone, she remarked that no child of nine could be censured for doing anything her mother told her. Which is one very good reason why the children of a divorced woman are taken away from her. Bel Fabian is not fit to have charge of any young creature. She is selfish, unprincipled, untruthful and a thoroughly bad example . . . Pamela, how *could* you let her get Alice—what possessed you? How did you come to meet her in the first place? Charles says he didn't introduce you. Is that true?'

'Yes, quite true. We saw her at Somerset House and I asked him who she was, that was all. She waylaid me a few days later when I was coming out of the jewellers.'

She told him how she had found Bel waiting in her carriage and he agreed that driving her to Harley Street had been almost unavoidable.

'But you should have left her at her door. There was no call to go inside. Why did you?'

'I liked her and I was sorry for her. I thought it must be so dreadful to be treated as an outcast.'

'Well, I can understand that,' he conceded. 'She can be very bewitching. What I can't understand is why you kept me in the dark. I thought I was in your confidence. Why didn't you tell me of this intriguing encounter?'

'I . . . I thought you might not be very pleased.'

'How astute of you. As it happens I am not very pleased, but I did not think you were afraid to risk my displeasure. Am I such an ogre?'

'No, of course not, Richard.'

She had not told him because she thought he would immediately launch an attack on Bel's character on evidence supplied by Decima. She did not want to tell him that either.

'So you went creeping off to Harley Street behind my back and let that harpy talk you into taking Alice there. How could you have been so irresponsible? You think the divorce laws cruel and unjust. They very often are, but you could at least have tried to find out the cause of this particular divorce. I could have told you that Bel committed adultery with three different men while her husband was fighting in Spain. She wept and made promises and pleaded with him until he forgave her. A few months later he actually caught her making love in a summer-house with her original seducer. Do you think she deserves much sympathy?'

Pamela was horrified, though after today she could believe almost anything of Bel.

She was still sufficiently prejudiced to ask, 'Did Decima tell you that?'

'No, she didn't. She never speaks of her brother's divorce. It was common knowledge.'

He watched her expression with a certain compunction, then came to sit beside her on the sofa.

'Poor Pam, you've had some shocks today, haven't you? It is easy to be taken in by experienced charmers like Bel and Charles. I suppose I should have looked after you more carefully. You may be a married lady, my darling, with two hopeful sons, but you are still only eighteen and a trifle young to fend for yourself in the jungle we call London society.'

'You do look after me, Richard,' she whispered, holding his hand. 'I'm sorry to have been so stupid.'

After all, he had provided her with an admirable woman friend, always ready with worldly and good advice. She had refused to listen and look what had happened.

'You will have to go and see Decima tomorrow and tell her how sorry you are for causing her so much worry and distress. She has been in the greatest suspense all day, not knowing whether we should catch up with Bel before they boarded the packet. Besides being very much attached to Alice and knowing how lost and uncomfortable she would be as a member of her mother's entourage in France, poor Decima also had hanging over her the necessity of having to tell her brother that his child had been abducted by his divorced wife. You must be able to enter into her feelings!'

'Oh, yes, I do understand. It was horrid for her. I know she disapproves of me, and she is perfectly right of course. After what has happened, I shouldn't think she will be able to bear the sight of me. Would it perhaps be better,' suggested Pamela in a very craven manner, 'if I apologised to her in a letter? One can express oneself more clearly in writing than in speaking.'

'No,' said Richard. 'It would not be better. After the way you have behaved you owe Decima the courtesy of calling on her in person, admitting yourself in the wrong, and telling her you are sorry. That is the least you can do. Not that she would refuse to accept a written apology, I'm sure she has no idea of exacting a penalty from you; it's I who won't accept it. I won't have my wife causing endless trouble for other people and then running away from the consequences because they may be unpleasant. I have some pride if you have none.'

He had let go of her hand and he was talking in a voice that sent icicles down her spine. She felt it was the voice he might have used on the morning of a battle to any young soldier who asked if he might leave the field because he wasn't feeling very well.

'You are right,' she said. 'I was running away. I'll go and see Decima in the morning.'

She was immediately rewarded. Slipping an arm round her, he said affectionately, 'That's my girl. It's always disagreeable having to eat humble pie, but it will soon be over.'

CHAPTER ELEVEN

RICHARD had been remarkably kind and forbearing. He was still in the same mood next morning when they walked round to Albemarle Street together.

'I think you'd better see Decima alone,' he said. 'I'll come with you if you wish, but this sort of occasion is generally more comfortable without an audience. And besides, we don't want to give the impression that you are under close arrest. I'll just look in on Hubert.'

Pamela agreed. If she had been obliged to go through this awkward meeting with anyone else in the world, she would have been glad of Richard's strong and supporting presence. As it was, she did not want him there when she was stumbling through her apologies to Decima, because, when it came to a comparison between them, she felt he was always on Decima's side. He might not be passionately in love with Decima—that was the one comparison she need not fear—but in regard to good breeding, sound judgement, unerring taste and delicacy of mind, she knew that Decima was Richard's idea of perfection.

They arrived at the Strangs and Richard gave her an encouraging smile as she prepared to follow the footman upstairs to the drawing-room.

She was formally ushered in. Decima rose, looking calm and composed and pretty in a becoming dress of coffee-coloured silk. Pamela advanced a little way into the room and stopped. They surveyed each other across a wide gap.

Pamela retained enough self-command to say, 'Decima, I'm so sorry.'

'I'm sure you are,' said Decima easily. 'Do come and sit down. Richard tells me you were completely deceived as to Bel's true character. I find this hard to understand myself, but I suppose I am prejudiced. I have every reason to dislike her.'

'Yes, I'm sure you must have. Any sister would feel as you do.'

Decima had been sewing. She picked up the tablecloth she was embroidering, an exquisite piece of whitework, and went on with her tiny, even stitches.

'It is a great pity you ever allowed yourself to become acquainted with Bel. To be visiting a divorced woman without Richard's knowledge or consent—that is a great deal more than most husbands would stand, I can tell you! However, that's no concern of mine, and I know you already resent what you consider to be my interference.'

She spoke without rancour and refrained from pointing out that in taking Alice to see her mother Pamela herself had been guilty of interference on a grand scale. But she was certainly thinking that and she had every right to.

With all the sincerity she could muster, Pamela said, 'I know I behaved very badly and I'm truly sorry to have caused you so much distress. I know you suffered hours of apprehension yesterday. I would have given anything to prevent that.'

'It was a groundless apprehension after all, so we need say no more about it.'

Decima smiled slightly and Pamela thought the worst was over. It had not been so bad after all.

But she was mistaken.

After a slight pause, Decima remarked, 'It is the damage you have done to poor little Alice which I find hard to forgive. The child has been crying almost incessantly since she came home.'

'Oh, no!' exclaimed Pamela, appalled. 'I thought she would be perfectly content once she understood that you were not going to blame her for what happened. She hadn't the slightest wish to go to France with her mother.'

'No, she wishes to go to her father in Devonshire. Unluckily George's health makes it impossible for her to live with him, and I hoped I finally persuaded her to accept the fact. When that wicked woman pretended they were going to Aldercombe, all her hopes were raised once more, only to be dashed. It is too bad. She will have to learn to bear the disappointment, but it has all been so unnecessary.'

'I am so very sorry,' said Pamela once again, wondering how many more times she would have to use this inadequate form of words. She really did mind about the harm she had done to Alice.

Searching around for some alleviation, she said, 'I expect Miss Stevens will find ways of diverting her. She is so good with Alice.'

'That is another annoyance. Alice will have to get used to a new governess. As soon as I can engage one.'

'What do you mean? What has happened to Mary Jane?'

'My dear Pamela, you cannot have thought I should go on employing Miss Stevens once I discovered she had been deceiving me. I dismissed her immediately and told her she must be out of the house within the hour.'

'I don't understand. How had she deceived you?'

'In exactly the same way that you had,' said Decima, speaking quite pleasantly. 'There was of course a very great difference in your situations. I am not able to dismiss you and I should not want to, for Richard's sake. Though I should prefer not to let you see too much of Alice in future. But Miss Stevens was an inmate of my own house, a paid servant in a position of trust. Of course she had to go.'

'But, Decima,' protested Pamela, aghast, 'Mary Jane never deceived you. She hadn't the faintest idea I was taking Alice to see her mother. I got her out of the way yesterday for that very reason. I didn't want to make things awkward for her so I asked her to go to Hatchard's. Didn't she tell you?'

'She lied to me, just as you are doing. Though perhaps you have more justification, for you do not want to have her dismissal on your conscience—I can see that. You made a favourite of her and I suppose it went to her head. You are not a very good judge of character, you must have realised that by now. Though I do think you ought to have learnt how to avoid being familiar with persons of an inferior station. You are married to a peer of the realm and you ought not to forget it.'

Pamela was so astounded and infuriated by this speech that she had no answer ready, but she stuck to the practical details which mattered most, and asked, 'Where did Mary Jane go? Has she any money?'

'I have not the faintest idea,' said Decima, carefully re-threading her needle. 'I suppose she will have to return to her father's parsonage, for no one will employ a governess who was dismissed without a character.'

'But she lives in Devonshire. She may not have enough for the fare.'

'She should have thought of that beforehand. If she is walking the streets of London, it is no more than she deserves. Though I don't think it at all likely. I expect she received a handsome bribe from Bel. It was Bel who first employed her, you know, at Aldercombe, and she must have known what was going on all the time she was there. I wanted George to replace her when they came to Bourne House, but he refused to make a change, saying Alice was used to her.'

With mounting incredulity Pamela realised that this self-righteous and complacent woman really did not like Mary Jane. Why? Presumably because Mary Jane did not like her, so she had jumped to the conclusion that there was some sort of squalid conspiracy which entitled her to ruin the prospects of the young governess by turning her adrift without a reference.

Pamela was suddenly overcome with anger. All good resolutions and humble apologies forgotten, she found herself on her feet, almost shouting.

'I never in my life met anyone so callous and unjust as you are. It was monstrous of you to condemn Mary Jane without a scrap of evidence, and worse still to turn her out of doors. Unchristian and unforgiving, even if she had betrayed your trust, which she didn't. She said so and I've said so, and I know that Richard believes me. But you won't. Because you can't ever admit you are in the wrong. What you suffer from is spiritual pride—which is quite as horrible as any sin of Bel's. And if your brother is at all like you, I'm not surprised she ran away from him. I sincerely pity her or anyone who is tied to a self-righteous hypocrite.'

She stopped because she had run out of breath. She still had plenty to say.

Decima had been sitting through the tirade apparently unmoved. Her colour did not change, and when she spoke her voice was soft and well modulated.

'Please try to regain command over your temper. These hysterical tantrums are very unbecoming, and if you do not learn to control them Richard will find himself saddled with a mad wife who is unfit to go out in society. I think you had better leave now before you say anything else you may regret later.'

Mention of Richard reminded Pamela of her primary grievance, the cause of all the trouble.

'You are very good at pronouncing on other women's reputations,' she said, her voice shaking. 'Your sister-in-law is immoral and I am mad. Perhaps you would care to hear what half London is saying about you!'

She got no further. The door opened behind her, and the butler announced, 'Miss Proudfoot and Miss Maria Proudfoot.'

Decima produced a rigid smile and managed to greet her new visitors with remarkable poise. They were two middle-aged sisters, generally known as the Proudfeet. Not very interesting in themselves, they made up for this by taking a great interest in everyone else. Pamela was aware of their curious glances and at the same time aware of herself and how she must appear, standing awkwardly in the middle of Decima's drawing-room and breathing hard, her face hot and red under the rosebush hat.

Before she could collect herself someone else entered the room and Richard was beside her.

'I'm afraid I shall have to drag you away, my dear,' he said with a touch of cool affectation, though meaning it literally. 'I know you will understand, Decima. We have an urgent engagement.'

He gripped Pamela's arm so hard that she almost cried out from the pain. She could never remember afterwards how she made her farewells or got down the stairs. In the hall stood Hubert, anxious and ineffective.

'I know you meant no harm, my dear,' he said, eyeing her mournfully. 'Alice must miss her mother, and how were you to know? But Dessy really is the best judge of Lady Bel's conduct. She has suffered so much from her already.'

Pamela wanted to explain that she had been defending Mary Jane, not Bel, but Richard did not give her the chance.

A second later they were out on the pavement and he was still holding her arm. She knew she had behaved very badly but she was too angry to care.

'Decima has treated Mary Jane abominably,' she said. 'Turned her into the street without a penny. Did you know that?'

'Hold your tongue,' he said quietly, 'and make some attempt at behaving yourself until I get you home.'

He did not speak again until they were back in Half Moon Street and in his study on the ground floor. Then he closed the door very deliberately and stood with his back to it as though she might try to escape.

'I would not have believed it,' he said, 'even of you. I thought I could rely on you to go upstairs and beg Decima's pardon for your criminal folly which nearly ended in disaster for Alice. You knew you were in the wrong, you knew how much trouble you had caused, yet you hadn't the grace to subdue your private hostility for the length of a morning call. Now you have made a public scene——'

'I don't know what you mean by public,' muttered Pamela.

'I mean that everyone in the house could hear you, including the servants and the children. I could hear you from the hall and so could those two women who will tattle about you all over town. I knew you could be very silly and childish—witness yesterday's performance—but I had not thought you could be so ill-bred.'

He looked her over with a fastidious dislike. There was a muscle jumping under the livid scar which gave him a bizarre and frightening appearance. She felt as though her knees were buckling under her and sat down in the nearest chair.

'I did apologise,' she told him. 'I said everything I ought. It was the way she spoke of Mary Jane that made me lose my temper. I don't think you understand. That poor girl has done nothing wrong and she has been turned away penniless.'

'It is you who don't understand. I had the whole story from Hubert.' Richard spoke with an icy precision. 'Decima assumed at first that Miss Stevens knew about the visit to Bel. Miss Stevens, not unnaturally, resented the accusation and seems to have spoken her mind a little too freely, which was a pity, because after that of course she had to go. I dare say they both regret their sharp words by now but the person chiefly to blame is yourself. As for her being left penniless, that is nonsense. Hubert paid her salary for the next quarter and also gave her the coach fare to Exeter.'

Pamela was crushed. It was impossible to go on championing Mary Jane as a friendless victim, exposed to the moral and physical dangers of a great city, and though it was kind-hearted Hubert, not Decima, who had ensured her safe return to her family, there was no point in saying so to Richard.

He was speaking again.

'You had better tell your maid to pack your trunks and give the same instructions to the nursery. I will deal with the servants. The house will be shut up and we shall start for Mallowdown in the morning.'

'For Mallowdown?' she repeated. 'Why?'

'Because I can't trust you to behave properly and I won't have you making an exhibition of yourself here. God knows the men of our family have created enough scandal, but the Cressinder ladies have always been irreproachable.'

She retained just enough spirit to say, 'If we leave town three weeks before the end of the session, won't that be the very thing to start people talking?'

'No matter if it does. They'll simply jump to the conclusion that you are breeding.'

She half imagined that she heard him add, 'It's the only thing you're fit for.'

CHAPTER TWELVE

PAMELA wandered along the edge of the ornamental canal in the July heat. Dragonflies shimmered on the surface of the water and along the opposite bank the marble figures of Roman emperors stood out dazzlingly white against the darkness of an ancient yew hedge. It was a beautiful scene and she was not able to enjoy it.

Richard had removed his family from London with the competence and skill of an old campaigner. He had spent one night at Mallowdown and then gone off to visit the Scarlet Hussars who were on manoeuvres in the New Forest. He had been gone a fortnight and he had not written to Pamela. She knew she was still in disgrace.

She was not surprised, for she knew it was all her own fault. She had been wrong to strike up a secret friendship with Bel Fabian, wrong in taking Alice to see her mother, and, if not actually wrong, extremely stupid to lose her temper with Decima when she had been meant to be apologising. She went hot and cold all over when she remembered what a scene she had made. Shrill and strident as a fishwife, shouting at Decima, who throughout the whole encounter had never once raised her voice. Decima had behaved like a lady, which Pamela emphatically had not. She could not wonder that Richard was disgusted with her.

Her only pleasant hours were spent with the twins, who were now able to sit propped up or roll about on a rug. Because there were two of them, they were more than twice as engaging as one baby would have been. Exactly alike, probably unaware that they were not the same person, yet puzzled by the number of arms and legs which all behaved differently. But she had to admit that, much as she loved them, she could not hold a conversation with her seven-month-old sons, and she was very lonely.

The London season ended without her and she heard that the Strangs were back at Bourne House though she did not see them.

Three days later Richard reappeared, brown and fit from his time in camp. The curricle overtook her while she was exercising the dogs in the avenue. Richard drew in the horses and got down to join her. He told Primrose to drive on to the stables; he would walk with her ladyship.

The curricle moved on. Richard and Pamela were left alone under the trees, the three spaniels floundering round them, overjoyed to see their master. In the informality of this arrival Richard and Pamela did not actually kiss, but he sounded quite affectionate as he asked her how she was, and how were the children? It was easy to talk about Rick and Roly and their wonderful signs of intelligence, a subject that lasted some time. Then it was his turn to say how much he'd enjoyed himself with the Scarlets.

"Do you wish you were still in the Army?" she asked rather wistfully.

"Not permanently. I don't think peacetime soldiering would suit me. But I must say it was good to be under canvas again, in fine weather and knowing, of course, that there was plenty to eat and no risk of a bullet through the head.'

She thought from his manner that he still remembered that dreadful morning in London as clearly as she did but was determined to behave generously and pretend he had forgotten. Later, while they were having dinner, he told her an amusing story about Hector Savage buying a horse which turned out to have been stolen.

He did not choose to sit with her in the summer parlour after dinner, only coming as far as the door to say, "Tomorrow we must drive over to call on the Strangs.'

She flushed, avoiding his eye. "Am I to come too? I thought you did not wish me to meet Decima.'

He frowned. "I thought Decima might not wish to meet you. That was why I brought you away from London in such a hurry. But I found a note from her waiting for me here. In it she points out that such near neighbours cannot afford to quarrel, and that if you and she were to avoid meeting there would be some unpleasant speculation. She is right, of course, and I hope you recognise that she is going out of her way to save you from criticism.'

It did just cross Pamela's mind that although rumours of her disgraceful behaviour might have gone ringing through the drawing-rooms of Mayfair, they were unlikely to have reached the country families who visited at Mallowdown and Bourne House. However, she had the sense to keep her mouth shut.

Presently she went to bed and lay in the darkness, straining her ears. She heard him go into the appartment he had occupied last year when she had been pregnant. He did not come out again. Obviously she had not been pardoned, simply bound over to keep the peace.

So she was in a highly nervous state when they arrived at Bourne House next day, fearing that almost anything she said or did might give a wrong impression to either Richard or Decima. She decided to keep as quiet as possible and hope she would not be accused of sulking.

She need not have worried. Decima took very little notice of her beyond saying with a false sweetness, 'I hope you have not come to apologise again, my dear Pamela. I don't think my nerves are equal to the strain.'

But this was only a passing shot for she had other things on her mind. Turning to Richard, she exclaimed, 'I am so glad you have come. I want you to talk to Hubert. You know how much he has been hinting lately about our removing to Yorkshire. Now he has got the bit between his teeth and nothing will satisfy him but we must all go and live there permanently. In that dreadful house I dislike so much, buried in the moors and miles from any good society.'

'I'm sorry to hear it,' said Richard. 'I can understand that Warby Hall must mean a great deal to him, but I can't see why he should want to settle there entirely.'

'That is what I keep saying. I am perfectly willing to spend a couple of months in the North every year; I should not regard that as too great a sacrifice. Anything more appears to me quite unreasonable. Why should we be uprooted from the happy and beautiful home I have made for him here, merely because he has a whim to revive the memory of his maternal ancestors? A set of ungenteel barbarians with nothing to recommend them beyond their great antiquity. They would be far better forgotten, if you ask me. And it is so unlike Hubert to take such a fancy. I wish you will speak to him, Richard.'

'I don't see that I can very well do that,' said Richard uncomfortably. 'If he wants my opinion, he is welcome to it, but I can't force him to listen to advice he hasn't asked for.'

Why not? wondered Pamela. You forced me to listen to a great deal of advice from Hubert's wife which I never asked for. Apparently the two cases were quite different.

'Then tell me this at least. Do you think I am making a great mountain out of a molehill?'

'Good heavens, no. I think it is abominable that you should be carried off to Yorkshire if you don't want to go. But don't despair, Dessy. You will be able to talk him round. You always do.'

Decima looked doubtful. She was not her usual confident self today, and in spite of everything Pamela felt a little sorry for her. Without the hard, enamel surface of her self-assurance, she seemed gentler, prettier. Was this the woman Richard and many other people saw all the time and found so charming?

The two old friends went on talking round and round the subject of Hubert's extraordinary obstinacy. They paid no attention to Pamela and she became bored and restless. They were sitting in the morning-room where there was a glass door opening straight into the garden. Presently she got up and slipped out.

She walked along the sunny terrace, thinking how blissful it would be if the Strangs went to live hundreds of miles away in Yorkshire. She did not feel very hopeful, however. Hubert had always been dominated by his wife, everyone said so. She remembered his telling her once about his mother's home in

Yorkshire and his wish to go and live there. He had not sounded as though he thought it would ever happen.

At the end of the terrace walk there was a shrubbery. The exotic plants and bushes were not making much of a show at present, this being the dull season between spring flowering and autumn berries, but there was a comfortable wooden seat at the heart of the green glade. Pamela went and sat on it.

She was still considering Hubert and Decima when a conspiratorial voice whispered, 'Lady Blaise!'

A small, slight figure stepped out from behind a lilac bush: Alice Fabian tiptoeing over the grass towards her.

Pamela had not seen Alice since the day of the abduction. She thought the child looked thinner and more withdrawn than ever and felt a sharp pang of guilt. Here was someone who had a genuine grievance against her.

Alice showed no sign of resentment. She came to sit beside Pamela and said confidingly, 'I'm so very glad to see you, Lady Blaise. I've been hoping to meet you ever since we came down from London, because there is something I want you to do for me, if you will. You don't mind my asking?'

'I will do anything I am able,' said Pamela rather doubtfully, being pretty certain that Decima would discourage any further association between herself and Alice.

'Oh, it is quite easy. I have written a letter to my papa and I want you to send it for me.'

Pamela gazed at her with concern. 'I can't do that. I don't know your papa.'

It was a silly thing to say, the best she could manage on the spur of the moment. Alice brushed it aside.

'You don't need to know him, only to get the letter posted. I can't do that from here because Aunt Decima will read it. She reads all my letters to Papa and makes me alter them and copy them out again. She says I must not tell him anything troublesome because he is not well. But I am sure it would not trouble him to have me at home and that is what I have said in this letter. Because it is horrid here now and I hate it. I want to go to Aldercombe.'

Pamela listened with growing dismay. She said, 'I'm afraid I did a very foolish thing in taking you to see your mama. Your Aunt Decima had every reason to be annoyed and upset, but she knew it was all my fault, and I hope you have not been punished, Alice, because of what happened.'

She waited anxiously for the reply.

'Oh, no, there wasn't any proper punishment. My aunt wasn't unkind. She never is. She just preached at me and made me feel a worm. Only she has sent my dear, dear Stevie away and the governess I have now is quite old and dreadfully strict. She doesn't know any interesting stories or exciting games and she watches me all the time as though they think I might run away. I expect I shall, too, if I can't get Papa to send for me. Dear Lady Blaise, you will post my letter, won't you? Here it is.'

She thrust a folded paper into Pamela's hand and at the same moment a large middle-aged woman could be seen approaching from the house, calling sharply, 'Alice! Alice!'

'I'll have to go,' said Alice regretfully. 'Otherwise she'll come spying on us.'

Diving into the bushes, she vanished briefly, and, when she reappeared, she was right on the edge of the shrubbery, where the new governess caught and scolded her. Pamela saw her being marched off to the schoolroom.

Poor little Alice, she thought, I've brought all this on her. She and Mary Jane are the real victims of my folly. If only I'd never laid eyes on Bel. Or, to be honest, if only I hadn't started scheming with Bel in order to steal a march on Decima. For that was the real cause of her fall from grace. She was still clutching Alice's letter to her father. What on earth was she to do about that? The last thing she wanted was to become further involved with the Fabian family, yet surely she owed Alice some sort of reparation. And there was that threat of running away if she didn't hear from her father. She couldn't mean it seriously. All the same ... Pamela put the letter in her reticule and strolled back to the house.

She was very silent on the drive home. Richard was silent too, though perhaps he expected some sort of comment from his wife, for after a while he said, defensively, 'It is hard on Decima to be asked to leave a place where she has been so happy.'

As though he were refuting an unspoken judgement that was bound to be unfavourable.

'Yes, I am sure she must feel it extremely,' agreed Pamela, who had not at that moment been thinking of Decima.

Back at Mallowdown, she shut herself in her dressing-room to read Alice's letter. She felt justified in doing this before deciding whether to send it to Colonel Fabian. The letter was simple and straight-forward, a child's longing for her father's affection with an undertone of acute homesickness. Alice said rather pathetically that she was not nearly so noisy and wild as she used to be and she promised not to be 'a newsense.' One particular paragraph made an impression on Pamela.

> My aunt says you will not be angry with me for seeing Mama. I only got in the carriage because I thought we were coming to Aldercombe. But she has sent Miss Stevens away which makes me very unhappy and it was not her fault either . . .

Pamela had Mary Jane Stevens very much on her mind, and would have liked to tell her so if she had known where to write. It was a country vicarage not far from Aldercombe but she had never heard the name of the parish. She knew she was responsible for ruining Mary Jane's prospects, because a governess who had been dismissed without a reference from her last employer could not hope to get another respectable situation. It now struck her for the first time that, strictly speaking, Mary Jane's last employer had been Alice's father. She had lived for some time at Aldercombe before the break-up of the Fabians' marriage and no doubt Colonel Fabian had gone on paying her salary while she was at Bourne House. If he had more sense of justice than his sister, Mary Jane would be entitled to give his name when applying for a new post. But only if he had been given a true version of the facts.

Pamela spent the afternoon composing a letter to Colonel Fabian. It was not at all easy admitting to a man she had never met that she was the imbecile who had taken his small daughter to see his divorced wife without the knowledge of her relations. She hoped he would not think that Richard had married a girl as heedless and immoral as Bel. Either that, or he must see me as an interfering busybody, which is probably nearer the mark, she thought gloomily. At least she was able to exonerate Miss Stevens and to assure George Fabian that Alice was a particularly quiet, thoughtful child, not likely to cause an uproar in the household of an invalid.

Having got all this down on paper, she was faced with a difficulty. How was she going to get the two letters into the post? The letters written at Mallowdown were placed on a table in the hall, collected every morning by the butler and taken by one of the grooms to the post office at Aulingford, where he would hand them in when he collected the incoming mail. Pamela knew that her epistle to Colonel Fabian would never pass unnoticed.

It was ridiculous that a person in her position could not achieve something as simple as posting a letter. But of course it was her position which made the whole business so awkward. Letters written by ordinary mortals were paid for by the recipients on arrival. Members of both Houses of Parliament were entitled to frank letters, which then travelled free. Richard franked all the letters which left Mallowdown as a matter of course. Pamela knew he would not approve of her writing to George Fabian behind Decima's back and enclosing a petition from Alice, yet if she addressed the letter herself and left it on the table, Thompson would point out that it had not been franked. He was very inquisitive and scrutinised all the letters; she had seen him doing it.

She thought of driving into Aulingford and going to the post office herself but she dared not risk it. She would almost certainly be recognised and soon there would be a story going round that Lady Blaise was posting letters to a gentleman which she dared not ask her husband to frank.

She was so absorbed by this problem that she sat through dinner without noticing that Richard was making friendly overtures and trying to amuse her. After a while he gave up, and she did not notice that either.

She was going to bed when a brilliant idea came to her. Why should she not frank the letter herself by imitating Richard's signature on the lower left hand corner? She would have to write out the whole address as though it were in his hand because that was required by law, but it should not be too difficult. Richard wrote in a quick positive way which suited his character, and, when it came to supplying franks for other people, he was inclined to scrawl.

Early next morning she sat down at her pretty little escritoire and started on her career as a forger. She wasted some paper and ink before she was satisfied, but finally achieved a cover, dashed off in a convincingly masculine hand, to Colonel George Fabian, Aldercombe Abbey, Exeter, Devonshire with the single name 'Blaise' in the corner. It was quite good enough to get past old Thompson.

CHAPTER THIRTEEN

DECIMA, not to be outdone in politeness, returned Pamela's call next day, bringing Hubert with her. It was not a happy occasion. Most of the talking was done by Decima and Richard. Pamela was afraid of saying the wrong thing, and Hubert sat and looked glum.

Since Decima's sense of propriety would not allow her to argue seriously with her husband in front of their friends, she treated the proposed move to Yorkshire as though it were a joke and pretended to tease him about it.

She tried to make Richard join in the fun, which embarrassed him, for Hubert was so clearly unamused. Presently she turned to Pamela.

'You always have an opinion of your own. How would it suit you to be dragged away from the Garden of Eden and taken to live in the wilderness?'

'Oh, I should be perfectly happy if that was what Richard wanted.'

Pamela answered so naturally and without hesitation that it must have been plain to everyone that she was speaking the truth, not studying for effect, trying to please Richard or annoy Decima.

Decima was annoyed at being made to appear a less than perfect wife. She attempted to get her own back by saying, 'It is easy for you to speak with such confidence. You've never cared much for this house, have you? You've never gone ahead with any of the improvements we decided on a year ago.'

Richard came to her defence. 'Pam hasn't had much time for improvements. She was only just recovered from her lying-in when we went up to town.'

Pamela felt a warm glow of triumph. It was the first time she ever remembered his taking her side against his admired Decima.

Decima flushed and bit her lip. Pamela glanced at Hubert and saw that he was looking miserable. It wasn't hard to guess the reason. Richard's wife had demonstrated that she loved him more than she loved his house. Decima, on the other hand, cared more for her surroundings than she did for her husband.

When the Strangs had gone, Pamela ventured to ask Richard, 'Why do you think she minds so much about going to Yorkshire? I should have thought that restoring a neglected estate would exactly suit her talents.'

'She dreads the isolation. You know she is very fond of society, which Hubert is not.'

'But surely they will have neighbours? I know there are many fine houses in the North of England.'

'Yes, but they are much further apart.'

Pamela was not so green as she had used to be, and she suddenly grasped the point. All those great Yorkshire families had been living there and inter-marrying through so many generations that no new-comer, however well born, could hope to gain the ascendancy which Mrs Strang of Bourne House had come to regard as her right. She had met with very little competition here. The two other important families in the neighbourhood were the Cressinders and the Carriswoods. The Carriswoods, though a good old county family, were inclined to be old-fashioned and provincial. As for the Cressinders, in spite of their ancient title they had been downright disreputable, and in any case there had been no Lady Blaise living during Decima's reign at Bourne House. Until Richard married me, thought Pamela. No wonder she tries so hard to keep me in my place. Or rather, out of my place. She did not say any of this to Richard.

She felt they were gradually coming together again. He had begun to talk to her about some improvements he wanted to make, not in the house but on the estate, and having lived all her life in the country she was able to show an intelligent interest in these.

The next few days passed pleasantly and then the blow fell.

They were on the point of going out riding together when a footman brought in the letters that had just been fetched from Aulingford. They were arranged on a silver salver which he offered first to Pamela, who took the single letter that was addressed to her. There was quite a pile for Richard, who accepted them and began to slit open the covers, glancing briefly at the contents until he came to one which fixed his attention.

'What an extraordinary thing! I don't know what he's talking about.'

'Who?' asked Pamela, looking up from a closely written page of her mother's doings in Bath.

'George Fabian. Something about Alice being unhappy and he supposes I must take the matter seriously as I provided the frank. I've never done such a thing in my life. I've often franked letters for Decima, though none just lately, and they none of them had anything to do with Alice. It's a mystery to me.'

Pamela was turned to stone. This was something she had not foreseen. She was half expecting that Colonel Fabian would reply directly to her, but this had not worried her, since Richard never made the slightest attempt to inspect her correspondence. It had not struck her that he would be more likely to consult Richard, his old friend and contemporary.

'As a matter of fact,' she began nervously, and then stopped because Richard was reading aloud.

'"Please thank your wife for her great kindness and assure her that her fears are groundless." Pamela! Have you been writing to Fabian? What the devil do you mean by it?'

'I had to. At least I felt I must. Alice was so anxious to get a letter to her father that had not been overseen, and then I thought I ought to explain that poor Mary Jane Stevens had done nothing wrong.'

'And the frank, how did that get there?'

'I—I copied your signature on the cover, Richard.'

'I might have guessed,' he said bitterly. 'You never learn, do you? Deceitful, mischief-making, indifferent to the feelings of others——'

'That's not true!' She flared up at the injustice. 'I was thinking only of Alice and Mary Jane.'

'Don't delude yourself,' he retorted. 'You were thinking of how much you could hurt Decima. That seems to have become your chief object in life. And going to the length of forging my signature... Don't you know that forgery is a capital offence?'

He had lost his sense of proportion along with his temper.

'Then you'd better see about getting me hanged. I'm sure you'd like to be rid of me. I can't think why you ever married me.'

'Oh, can you not?' he enquired, on a dangerous note of sarcasm which she failed to recognise because by now she too had lost her temper.

'You came down to Crewse and forced yourself on me and my parents, knowing nothing whatever about me except what you must have guessed: that I was very ill-equipped to become the sort of wife you wanted: a great lady, the mistress of your baronial mansion and a fashionable hostess, the perfect copy of Decima. You could have found any number of women like that, standing around the ballroom at Almack's, dying to be asked for. Why did you have to offer for me? I certainly did nothing to encourage you.'

She was possessed by fury and resentment which had for the time cast out all other emotions.

Richard looked across the room at her, his face hard, the scar jumping again and that suggestion of menace she had almost forgotten.

'You want to know why I married you?' he said in a deadly quiet voice. 'Very well, then. I'll tell you. Your father trapped me into it.'

She drew a sharp breath. 'I don't believe you.'

'Whether you believe me or not is of no consequence. That is what happened. He wrote, inviting me to Crewse, and pointing out that although we had not met, we were distantly connected because my great-aunt Lady Emden had been your godmother.'

Pamela sat listening with a sudden sinking dread of what she was going to hear.

'It's true I was looking for a wife,' he said, 'but I had not committed myself in any way when I came to Crewse. When I arrived you were nowhere to be found. It was perfectly obvious you were trying to avoid me, and by the time your mother produced you for my inspection, sulky and reluctant, I had made up my mind that we should not suit. And then, after dinner, your father took me into his confidence. He told me of his financial losses, adding that he and your mother had been prepared to face their altered situation without too much regret while they believed that you would be safely provided for as Lady Emden's heiress. She had made a will in your favour some years before and told them all about it. He begged me to picture their dismay when they found that everything was left to me instead. And he did not fail to point out that I hardly needed Lady Emden's bequest, since I had just inherited a fortune of my own.'

'How *could* he?' whispered Pamela.

'He was desperate, my dear. He did not know what was to become of you, so he talked me into marrying you as a matter of conscience.'

Richard laughed sardonically. 'You must remember that I had grown up as a younger son. I wasn't used to the tactics of matchmaking parents. He even told me you might have to go for a governess—a daunting thought. How long do you think you'd have lasted in that profession? I'm sure you're better off as a married woman. Even married to me. Governesses, as you know, are not allowed to make mistakes.'

Pamela got up quickly and left the room.

She was able to control herself long enough to run upstairs and find the privacy of her bedchamber. There she flung herself on the bed and sank into a flood of tears. 'How could he?' she sobbed, not knowing whether she meant Richard or her father or both.

She recognised that her papa had done what he thought was best in his bumbling way, yet she almost hated him for the humiliation he had caused her. To learn that Richard had simply married her out of pity! All through their various difficulties she had found comfort in believing that if she were a disappointment to him, it was not her fault. She had not gone out of her way to catch such an eligible husband, she had not even wanted to marry him; it was no one's fault but his own. Now it turned out that he had acted out of mistaken chivalry. So perhaps he was entitled to try and change her into the sort of girl he had really wanted to marry. A wife created in the image of Decima but one who was already fitted to play the part without Decima's tuition.

Well, he had fallen in love with her all the same. Or had he? She began to doubt that too. *She* had fallen in love, headlong and without reserve. Richard had found her intensely desirable during those happy weeks in London, she was sure of that. He had been a demanding lover, a delightful companion, they had laughed and rejoiced together—but wasn't that just the charming way he would have treated his mistresses in the years before he settled down? In her misery she even wondered whether her response to him had been too passionate, too abandoned, not the sort of conduct a nobleman expected from a wife he had married by arrangement because he needed an heir.

Decima would never have surrendered to such emotions. Pamela had known this all along and congratulated herself on the difference between them. Here, too, perhaps she had been wrong.

She lay on her bed all through a hot afternoon, her whole body aching, her skin damp and feverish.

When Toller came in to lay out her dress for dinner, she said at first that she was ill and would not come down. Then she changed her mind. It was no good hiding away and giving Richard even more reason to despise her.

She dressed and crept downstairs, knowing only too well that her eyelids were red and swollen, but he hardly looked at her, so perhaps he did not notice. They dined in silence. Pamela could not help remembering their first meal in that room, when they had driven to Mallowdown immediately after their wedding. She had been frightened of Richard then, with the natural apprehension of a bride on her wedding night, exaggerated by the fact that they were practically strangers, that she still thought herself in love with someone else and all sorts of vague Gothic fancies hovered round his gloomy house, the reputation of his family, and that disfiguring scar. Her fears had been quite ridiculous. She could not imagine what she had thought Richard would do to her. Her introduction to marriage had been very uncomfortable, but only because she had not known how to respond.

She had long ago realised that Richard could never be physically cruel to anyone weaker than himself. Yet here she was, afraid of him again, and it was worse than before. He could hurt her merely by the cruel things he said and she had no defence against him.

She was desperately vulnerable because now she loved him.

The covers were removed, the dessert set on the table; painted plates, dishes piled with raspberries and apricots, decanters of port and brandy. It was all very slow and laborious.

At last the servants left them alone. Pamela felt she ought to offer some sort of apology, for writing to George Fabian, for losing her temper when she knew she was in the wrong, most of all for marrying him. Though she did not think she could put all this into words.

So she simply said, 'I'm sorry.'

'Yes, you always are,' said Richard coldly. 'There is not much sense in discussing the matter.'

CHAPTER FOURTEEN

PAMELA hardly saw Richard during the next few days. He breakfasted early, took himself off, perhaps to Bourne House, and did not come home until after dinner.

The third morning was particularly hot and sunny. It was the day of the Aulingford Fair, a great local event for all classes. Besides the ordinary booths and sideshows there would be a cricket match and fireworks in the evening. Pamela had missed the fair last year on account of her pregnancy. This year Richard had said they would go together, but she was sure he had changed his mind. Once again he had disappeared.

The Strangs were going *en famille*. Decima had promised to take the children, and, so that they could see the fireworks and then go immediately to bed, she had accepted an invitation for them all to stay the night with friends who had a large house on the edge of the town.

Pamela was wandering aimlessly in the grounds just before midday when she caught a distant glimpse of a carriage approaching along the road that ran between Bourne House and Mallowdown. This must be the Strang family on their way to the fair. She wondered if Richard was with them. In a few minutes the carriage would pass the Mallowdown gates. She was drawn irresistibly downhill to a place in the shade of a grove of trees where she could watch unseen as her neighbours drove by.

The Bourne House barouche had the hood down, so it was easy to see everyone inside. Decima and the new governess were sitting with little Dessy between them, Alice facing them with her back to the horses. Hubie had been allowed to sit on the box beside the coachman and Nurse was up there too, to make sure he did not fall. There were no accompanying riders, no sign of either Richard or Hubert.

She watched the barouche disappear behind a curtain of fine, feathery dust. She was ashamed of coming here to spy. It was a degrading thing to have done and she hadn't even the excuse of believing that Richard and Decima were actually lovers. Though it seemed odd to her that this one omission rendered them perfectly innocent in the eyes of Church and State. Richard's open admiration and preference for Decima did not count as infidelity, even if it hurt and distressed his wife more than an occasional secret adultery would have done.

She thought suddenly of the Charles Everards. She had been very much shocked when they discovered Lord Charles on the way to France with Bel. It seemed a wicked betrayal of Emily. Yet apparently she knew about his love-affairs and remained devoted to him, always giving an impression of happy serenity. Lord Charles certainly thought the world of her and it was delightful to see them together. In spite of his wayward conduct Charles Everard valued his wife more highly than any other woman. Richard did not.

I'd almost rather be her than me, thought Pamela bitterly.

The day passed slowly. The house seemed un-
bearably quiet—quieter than usual because it was an
understood thing that as many as possible of the servants would be given leave to go to the fair. A few of
the older ones stayed in by choice and they provided
Pamela with her solitary dinner. The nursery party
was high up on the second floor. Otherwise the house
was empty.

Pamela sat alone in the summer parlour, trying to
read a novel. It was not very interesting and presently
she fell asleep.

She was woken some hours later by the sound of
voices and sat up, wondering where she was. Not in
her bedroom; the candles were in the wrong places
and she was cold and stiff. Then she remembered.

Turning, she saw an extraordinary vision in the
doorway: Thompson the butler, not in his sober black
as she was used to seeing him, but in trousers and
shirt, hurriedly pulled on, and wearing a nightcap.
Pamela stared. Was she still asleep and dreaming or
had he come home drunk from the fair?

His manner when he spoke was punctilious though
he was clearly upset. 'I beg your pardon, my lady. I
did not mean to intrude on your ladyship, but, seeing
a light under the door, I thought his lordship must
be here. It is a matter of the greatest urgency.'

'But what's happened, Thompson? What time is
it?'

'Half-past one, my lady. And this young man has
ridden over from Bourne House on purpose to find
his lordship.'

She had come to the door and saw behind him a
fresh-faced young countryman in boots and breeches
who looked vaguely familiar. At the same moment

another door opened, and Richard's voice, coming from the Spanish parlour, demanded, 'What the devil's going on?' He advanced towards them, holding high a branched candlestick. 'Who's that with you, Thompson?'

'One of the grooms from Bourne House, my lord.'

'Oh, yes. Poole, isn't it? What is it you want?'

'If you please, my lord, Mr Beckley sent me, because he didn't know what he ought to do. It's the master, my lord. He's dead.'

'Dead!' repeated Richard. 'How is it possible? He was perfectly well yesterday. Has there been an accident?'

Pamela heard herself cry out in shocked astonishment. Hubert dead. She could not believe it. She felt, not faint exactly, like some silly swooning female, but as though her mind had come adrift from her body and everything seemed a long way off.

The young groom was saying that the master hadn't been taken ill as far as they knew, and it didn't seem like an accident.

'We'd all been to the fair. We came back in the waggon, the house servants went indoors, and Mr Beckley, that's the butler, my lord, I expect you know—took a look round, and it was he found the master, lying down like as he might be asleep, only he was dead and cold. And all alone in the house.'

'Then where was Mrs Strang?'

'I think she and the children are staying with the Vincents in Aulingford,' Pamela reminded him. 'That's what she intended.'

'So she did. I'd forgotten.'

Richard was too preoccupied to be surprised at finding his wife dressed and downstairs in the middle of the night.

'And I don't think Hubert can have gone to the fair,' she added. 'I happened to catch sight of the barouche as it was driving past and he wasn't with them.'

'That's right, my lady,' said the groom. 'Mr Beckley said he changed his mind at the last moment but wouldn't stand in the way of any of the servants going. A very kind gentleman he always was.'

'Yes, he was,' said Richard. 'This is terrible news. I'll go straight over to Bourne House now. You'd better press on to Aulingford, Poole, and fetch the apothecary. If he isn't best pleased—and he won't be at this hour—tell him I sent you.'

'Yes, my lord.'

Pamela made a tentative offer. 'Would you like me to come with you, Richard?'

'I don't see what good that will do.' Pamela was humbly ready to accept this estimate of her usefulness, when Poole spoke up unexpectedly.

'When I came away, a few of the young women were in a fair way to having the vapours. Mrs Bower might be glad to have a lady on the premises.'

'Oh, well, in that case...'

Richard did not want a houseful of hysterical maidservants on his hands. He said quite gratefully that he would be glad to take Pamela with him.

They hardly spoke on the way to Bourne House. Richard had no attention to spare from the strain of driving at night, and Pamela was thinking of Hubert, whom she had come to like in spite of never finding him an amusing or stimulating companion. He was good and steady and fair-minded—no need to call these virtues dull, and the idea of his death saddened her. Disturbed her, too, for at her age she did not expect people to die, and a man as reliable and unassuming as Hubert had become so much a part of the background of her life that she would almost have counted on his being there forever. If anyone had to die, it seemed strange that Hubert, the least volatile of men, should have left them so suddenly and without warning.

She felt genuinely sorry for Decima. It must be dreadful to be left a widow and they had always seemed a harmonious couple. Until lately, at least. It flashed into her mind that now Hubert was dead Decima would not go Yorkshire. She would stay here and go on convincing Richard of her own perfection and his wife's inferiority.

Pamela dutifully steered her mind away from this selfish reflection.

Arrived at Bourne House, they found the front door open and the butler waiting anxiously in the hall. He conducted them into the library, which had a rather strange appearance, for all the candles and wall-sconces were lit, though the shutters had not been closed or the curtains drawn.

Pamela hardly noticed this; she was so startled by the sight of Hubert's body stretched out face downwards on the floor. She had imagined his dying quietly in his chair. Richard leant down to touch his cheek.

'He's been dead for hours. Was everything like this when you found him, Beckley?'

'Except for the lights, my lord. The room was in darkness. I came in here to make sure that the windows were fastened, and I nearly stumbled over him. He was already cold. That's how I knew for certain he was dead.'

And presumably he had then obeyed a deep instinct by surrounding his master's body with lights.

While the men were talking, Pamela had moved a little nearer. She could not see much of Hubert's face from the way he was lying, only the angle of brow and cheek. The skin was deathly white—yes, literally deathly—but his folded arms were propping his chin and the rest of his features were hidden. His head was resting in what looked like a comfortable position on a large red cushion from one of the library armchairs.

Pamela found she was crying. She gulped back her tears. Richard put a comforting arm round her and tried to draw her away, but there was something she wanted to know.

'Did you put the cushion under his head, Beckley?'

She thought he must have done so when he had lit the candles.

'No, my lady. He was lying just as he is now when I came in.'

'Very odd,' said Richard.

They gazed about the room. There were several piles of books on the writing-table. These had apparently come from the highest of the shelves that ran up the wall. The neat mahogany library steps were drawn up just below. On a small table next to an old, friendly armchair was a tray with an empty glass on it and a brandy decanter which was also nearly empty. Richard looked thoughtfully at the decanter but made no comment.

Instead he asked, 'Is it true that your master was entirely alone in the house until you and the other servants returned from the fair? An invitation to thieves, surely?'

The butler hastened to explain. At Bourne House, as at Mallowdown, it was the custom that everyone who could should go to the fair. For safety's sake a couple of men were always left on guard, and this year it had been two of the gardeners who had been put in charge. They had been sitting up in one of the outside pavilions when the servants returned. They swore they had patrolled the house regularly during the evening, but they had not gone inside. They had no reason to.

'I see,' said Richard. 'Why didn't Mr Strang go to Aulingford with his family? Did he tell you? Could he have been feeling ill?'

'I doubt that, sir. He said he was too busy checking the library catalogue. I fancy,' remarked Beckley, with the wooden expression of a butler who knew more than he was willing to admit, 'that this had some connection with the family's proposed move to Yorkshire. Of course it would have been proper for some of us to have remained behind, but he wouldn't hear of it. He said he didn't need hot meals on such a day and if we left enough cold food in the diningroom he would help himself.'

'And how much of the food did he eat?'

'I don't know,' said Beckley, taken aback. 'I didn't think to look.'

'Then perhaps you would go and see.'

As Beckley withdrew, Pamela asked Richard what he thought had happened.

'Do you think Hubert had a seizure?'

'It doesn't look like that to me. The way he is lying, with that cushion under his head—as though someone had arranged the body after death.'

'And left him lying face downwards?' Pamela shuddered. 'Who could have done such a thing? The house was empty.'

'Well, that's just it. Suppose someone broke in— those gardeners can't have been watching all the time—there's no visible sign of an injury but he might have received a blow on the back of the head. We shall know more about that when Williams arrives.'

He was interrupted by Beckley, who returned from the dining-room to say, 'He never touched any of the dishes that were set out for him. There's not so much as a crumb on the cloth or a used plate!'

'Was that decanter full this morning?' Richard glanced towards the small table.

'Yes, my lord. I can't understand it. He wouldn't— he was a most abstemious gentleman.'

'I know. He wouldn't have drunk so much brandy in the middle of the day and on an empty stomach.'

But if a thief had got in, thought Pamela, expecting to find the house empty, he might have been surprised by the owner and killed him in a moment of panic. And after such a deed, he might very well have drunk the brandy to steady his nerves. But would he have placed a cushion under his victim's head before escaping? The idea was fantastic.

Mrs Bower, the housekeeper, came in, demanding that the master's body should be carried upstairs, or at least laid on a sofa in a properly respectful manner.

'...Not left on the floor, as though we were all a pack of heathens. It does seem so dreadful, my lord, just to let him lie there as if we no longer cared to do our duty towards him now he's dead. And what Madam is going to say when she hears, poor lady, I can't bear to think.'

'Your feelings do you credit,' said Richard soothingly, 'but I should like Mr Williams to take a look at him before he is moved. He should be here very soon. In the meantime, I have brought her ladyship with me, in case you need any help in dealing with the maids.'

He shot Pamela a speaking glance and gave the tearful housekeeper a gentle push in her direction.

Pamela got Mrs Bower out of the library before she broke down. In fact none of the maids was in the least hysterical. They had simply been over-excited when they got back from the fair and were plunged into an atmosphere of tragedy.

It was Mrs Bower who needed calming. Pamela made several unsuccessful efforts and then had an inspiration. She said she was very thirsty and would like a cup of tea.

Mrs Bower instantly became competent and sensible. She lit the spirit-kettle and produced china cups and saucers from her dresser in the housekeeper's room, and after a slight protest was persuaded to sit down at the table with Pamela and drink tea in an atmosphere of bizarre gentility.

While they sat, the housekeeper talked on and on about what a shocking thing it was, and what Madam was going to say, and how she and Madam had always agreed in thinking it a very foolish custom that all the servants should be sent off to the fair and the house left unattended. Madam had wanted them to take turns, year by year, only the master wouldn't hear of it. He insisted that everyone should have the chance to go because that was how it had been in his father's day.

So Hubert did have occasional victories, thought Pamela.

Mrs Bower, though devoted to her master, could not help pointing out how sensible Decima had been about the fair.

'For if some of us had been here, this would never have happened,' she declared in a voice of gloomy triumph though without much evidence. 'And, besides, all this gallivanting is bad for the young servants. Here's Betty now, the second housemaid, left behind in Aulingford and the dear knows what mischief she's been getting into, though most of us can guess, and Madam will never countenance anything of *that* nature.'

Mrs Bower continued her monologue while the dawn crept up the sky and somewhere in the house Richard conferred with the apothecary.

At last he came to tell her that he was ready to take her home. He would then drive on himself to the house where Decima and the children were staying in Aulingford and get her hostess Mrs Vincent to break the sad news of her husband's death.

'What did Williams say?' Pamela asked when they were once more in the curricle.

'There was no sign of violence, no bruise or contusion of any sort, but he doesn't think it was a natural death either. The whole thing's damned odd. He says—I can hardly believe this—he says it looks like some sort of opiate poisoning.'

'Good gracious!' exclaimed Pamela. She was half asleep but this jerked her back to full attention. 'How could he have been poisoned, poor Hubert? And who would want to do such a wicked thing?'

'I imagine Williams was thinking of some unlucky accident. God knows what we are to tell Decima.'

CHAPTER FIFTEEN

PAMELA spent a few hours in bed, and when she came downstairs she was still feeling bemused, either from sleep or the lack of it. While she was having a late breakfast, she was told that Primrose was waiting to speak to her.

'Tell him to come in.'

Richard's personal groom entered the breakfast-room and stood to attention in a soldierly manner.

'Good morning, Primrose,' she said, smiling. 'Have you a message for me? Where's his lordship?'

'Good morning, my lady. The colonel instructed me to tell you that he is accompanying Mrs Strang to Bourne House and will remain as long as she has need of him.'

'Yes. I see. Thank you.'

Primrose went on standing there, so that she thought he had something else to say to her, but he remained silent. Speaking at random, she asked whether Mrs Strang was taking the children home with her.

'I believe not, my lady. I was told in the servants' hall that they were to stay on in the care of Mrs Vincent. I understand that Mrs Vincent offered to go to Bourne House with Mrs Strang but she refused.'

Primrose was gazing so hard at Pamela as he said this that she felt sure he was trying to convey some kind of information which it would not be proper for him to put into words. It took her only a few seconds to grasp what this was. Decima was a new-made widow who was returning home without the protection of her children's presence or a female friend, and with Richard as her only companion. He had been accustomed to come and go as he pleased at Bourne House while Hubert had been alive. His doing so now was bound to cause talk.

Pamela saw at once what she ought to do. She did not want to, and they would not want her and would probably make her feel uncomfortable, but that couldn't be helped.

She said, 'I must call on Mrs Strang and see if I can be of any help to her. Will you drive me over, Primrose?'

'Yes, my lady,' said Primrose, looking much relieved.

He had looked after Richard all through the war, saving his life, so Richard himself declared. Now he was as determined as a dowager to save his master's reputation. Dear Primrose, thought Pamela, sitting beside him in the curricle, What a nice man he is. Though she could wish he had not been quite so protective and she was feeling very uneasy by the time they reached Bourne House, afraid that Richard would misunderstand her reason for coming.

Shown into the small drawing-room, she found Richard and Decima seated side by side in earnest conversation. They looked round at her in evident surprise.

'My dear Pam,' exclaimed Richard, getting up. 'I did not mean to bring you over here. Did you mistake my message?'

He did not sound cross, merely tactless.

Ignoring him, Pamela turned to Decima. 'I had to come, to see if there was anything I could do. I am so very, very sorry.'

It struck her that every time she met Decima now she had to begin by saying she was sorry. The thing was becoming a farce. Though, of course, her reason for being sorry this time was far more creditable.

The two women embraced awkwardly, both knowing it was the right thing to do on such an occasion. Decima was very pale. She must have changed her dress since arriving home, for she was already wearing black. Who but Decima would have a black dress ready to hand? Of course, she had been in mourning for her mother-in-law last year.

'Thank you, Pamela. It is so kind of you to offer.'

Her voice was husky, there was a handkerchief screwed tightly in her hand and a vinaigrette on the table beside her. Otherwise no sign that she had been weeping.

'And you have already been here a great part of the night,' she added, as Pamela sat down. 'I hear you were a great comfort to poor Bower.'

Supporting the housekeeper is all I'm fit for, thought Pamela, though she did not think Decima meant to sound condescending. She just could not help it.

'I think the servants needed support in such a situation. They were so anxious to do what you would wish without knowing exactly how.'

'Yes, I am aware of that,' said Decima in a low voice. 'Poor Hubert, it is dreadful to think of his being here all alone. I simply cannot make sense of what happened. Why did he not follow us to Aulingford? He was not very anxious to come, which is why we started without him, but he did not positively decline. If he was feeling ill, why didn't he say so?'

They heard the sound of hoofbeats and the crunch of gravel outside and a moment later Beckley was announcing Mr Carriswood. Pamela was profoundly thankful she had come. It had been worth risking a snub.

Bonham Carriswood, besides being a large land-owner, was a Justice of the Peace, keenly interested in the death of a brother magistrate. Having paid his formal condolences to Decima, he asked if he might speak to her alone. He had a serious intelligence to communicate. A bluff, downright character as a rule, he spoke like this because he was embarrassed.

'Well, please tell me what it is,' said Decima 'I should prefer Lord and Lady Blaise to remain.'

'As you wish, ma'am.' Mr Carriswood cleared his throat. 'I regret to tell you that Williams is of the opinion your husband did not die a natural death. He suspects an overdose of laudanum.'

Rather pale now, Decima said, 'Lord Blaise prepared me for this, but I simply don't believe it. Where would Hubert have found any laudanum? And what reason could he have for taking any? I hope you are not implying that he indulged in that nasty, vicious habit.'

'Certainly not, Mrs Strang. But there is always the possibility of an accident. Could he not have helped himself to laudanum in mistake for some other physic?'

'No, he couldn't, because I don't keep any in the house. I've always considered it highly dangerous. Williams has prescribed it from time to time, diluted in a stomach mixture or a soothing syrup for a bad cough. I've always taken charge of such medicines myself and thrown them away as soon as the patient recovered.'

There was a thoughtful pause. Richard was getting ready to speak when Carriswood asked, 'Is there anyone in the house with a grudge against your husband? A disgruntled servant who might have played a spiteful trick without considering the consequences? Someone who was under notice of dismissal, for instance.'

'No one. Our servants stay with us for years, and they are all well-behaved and respectable. At least,' Decima added after a slight hesitation, 'I may be obliged to get rid of my second housemaid. My housekeeper tells me she did not return from the fair with the other servants.'

Pamela noted that the unfortunate Betty was not back yet, and, despite the tragedy in her own life, Decima had managed to get the truth out of Mrs Bower and pass judgement.

Richard was saying, 'All this talk of poison seems to be a little hasty. Williams has nothing to go on but suspicion.'

'Exactly.' Mr Carriswood shifted unhappily. His fingers beat a tattoo on the arms of his chair, and he avoided looking at any of his companions. 'As things are, it appears to be a matter for the coroner. Very disagreeable for all concerned. Now if Mrs Strang were to give permission for a post-mortem examination, Williams would probably find the true cause of death and there would be no need of an inquest.'

At this suggestion Decima lost some of her remarkable self-command.

'Oh, no!' she exclaimed in a painfully agitated voice. 'Poor Hubert—I could not endure such a desecration!'

Richard said soberly, 'If there is an inquest, I'm afraid the coroner might insist on an autopsy.'

Pamela was moved by a spontaneous feeling of sympathy. Reaching out to take Decima's cold hand, she said, 'Don't you think Hubert may have had something wrong with him which no one was aware of? A fatal weakness of the heart, perhaps. You know my father suffers greatly from that condition. He is an invalid now, but the first onset took us entirely by surprise. If you allow this horrid examination, the surgeons may be able to set your mind at rest.'

Decima gave her an unseeing glance, but then said, 'I dare say you are right. It would be better to know.'

On their way home Richard said to Pamela, 'It was well done of you to mention your father's illness. The suggestion of a chronic disease was the one thing that could have persuaded Decima to agree to the post-mortem.'

'I hope I didn't mislead her. I can't imagine any of Papa's attacks ending quite like that.'

If her father ever had such a spasm when he was quite alone, he would fall heavily, probably disarranging the furniture, and be found sprawling and ungainly—the picture made her shudder. He was not likely to lie down on the floor as though preparing for sleep. Of course many people did die in their sleep, but not on the library floor.

'I know what you're thinking,' said Richard, 'but the point is, Decima agreed to a post-mortem of her own free will, instead of being obliged to do so after a public inquest. If only they find a satisfactory cause of death, there will not have to be an inquest after all. She will have you to thank for that.'

Pamela felt a glow of pleasure and her eyes filled with tears. She despised herself for this weakness. It was ridiculous, pathetic even, to be so grateful for any crumb of praise. And on such an impersonal subject too. Well, it was the only appreciation she was going to get from Richard now, an occasional tribute to the useful action or sensible remark a man ought to be able to count on from a wife whom he had married without love because he had been forced into it.

Her body ached for him as she remembered rapturous embraces and tender, laughing glances, but their eyes slid past each other now and they never touched.

Even her recommending the post-mortem defeated its own object, because Bonham Carriswood called next day to announce that Hubert Strang had had nothing organically wrong with him; he had died from swallowing an excessive quantity of laudanum and brandy.

Pamela wanted to ask, How could they tell? But she thought better of it. She was not particularly squeamish herself but thought Mr Carriswood probably was.

'I simply don't understand it,' said Richard. 'If Strang wasn't ill or in pain, why would he take laudanum? He certainly wasn't addicted to the stuff. And where would he have got it? Mrs Strang swore there was none in the house.'

'She says so still, though we have now found the receptacle.'

He pulled out of his pocket a small cut glass bottle, cylindrical in shape, with a cork in the top and a little fluid still inside.

'That had laudanum in it. The servants found it under the bureau in the library. They weren't able to get in there to clean until the body had been removed. I suppose it had rolled out of sight.'

'But where did it come from?' Pamela wondered. 'Doesn't Mrs Strang know?'

'Never seen it before, apparently.'

They all stared down at the bottle which Mr Carriswood had put down on the table. It was rather smaller than the usual glass containers which men and women alike kept on their dressing-tables.

'It belongs to a fitted travelling-case,' said Richard. 'There are bottles very like that in the one I took to Spain with me. I've got it still.'

'Have you?' Carriswood straightened up, frowning 'Could I see it, Blaise?'

'If you wish.'

They were in the Spanish parlour. Richard pulled the bell-rope and sent a servant to find his old wartime dressing-case. There was a curious lapse into silence as though no one were breathing. At last Richard's valet appeared, bringing the travelling-case. It was a small wooden chest with brass handles and a brass inlay, which must have been extremely elegant and was still well polished, though the wood had been cracked and scratched in several places during Richard's lengthy journey up the Spanish peninsula. There was a brass panel on the lid inscribed, 'Captain the Honourable Richard Cressinder XXVIIth Hussars,' which showed how long Richard had owned it.

'Thank you, Clayton,' he said. 'Put it here on the table, will you? Is that the key?'

He unlocked the case, revealing a nest of dark blue velvet, somewhat scuffed and faded with various hollows, cavities and grooves designed to hold steady brushes, combs, razors, boxes, jars and bottles. There should have been three of the latter but only one remained. It was a duplicate of the one found at Bourne House, even to the pattern of the cut glass. It had a silver stopper engraved with his family crest, a swan *passant*.

'I think the other two were broken when this thing fell off a mule while we were crossing the Pyrenees,' he said. 'I'd forgotten that.'

Carriswood leant across and removed the silver screw top from the bottle from Bourne House. It fitted perfectly.

'Are you sure both bottles were broken in the Pyrenees?'

'I think so. It's a long time ago.'

'You did not take this one to Bourne House at any time?'

'Of course not. Why should I?'

Mr Carriswood did not answer. Soon afterwards he left.

Richard could barely contain himself long enough to see the magistrate off the premises. He came back to Pamela, seething.

'That fool was suggesting I poisoned Hubert!'

'Oh, surely not?' she said feebly.

'I don't know what else he could have meant. And while they were fetching his horse he had the impertinence to ask me where I was yesterday and why he hadn't seen me at the fair.'

Pamela had been wondering the same thing though not for the same reason.

'What did you tell him?' she ventured.

Richard shrugged. 'I said I was riding about the woods. It was no business of his.'

Pamela thought he had kept away from the fair because he was too angry to take her with him yet did not wish to be seen there without her. Naturally he would not care to explain this, so his actions were bound to raise suspicion in anyone who felt there was something to suspect. She racked her brains for something helpful to suggest.

'He was misled by the odd circumstance of the matching bottles. But if you had taken laudanum over to Bourne House in that little flask, you would never have mentioned your dressing-case or allowed him to see it. No one in his senses could have been so rash.'

'Very sound reasoning,' said Richard drily, 'but do you think friend Carriswood will be able to work that out for himself?'

CHAPTER SIXTEEN

THERE was now no avoiding an inquest and this was held two days later at Bourne House. Richard absolutely refused to take Pamela with him. She wanted to go because she was afraid he might have unpleasant questions to answer. He refused to take her, probably for the same reason,

As it turned out, however, he was not asked about the bottles in his dressing-case. The coroner merely enquired about his being summoned to Bourne House in the middle of the night, and what he did when he got there.

Decima gave evidence that her husband had been in good health and good spirits, Beckley and several other servants supported this, and then there was the medical evidence.

The jury returned a verdict that Mr Hubert Strang had died from swallowing a large quantity of laudanum, there being insufficient evidence as to the circumstances in which it had been administered.

Richard told Pamela all this, adding that the cortège with Hubert's body would start for Yorkshire tomorrow. Ironically he was going to be buried among his mother's ancestors and sleep until the end of time in the place where he had so longed to live.

'Will Decima go up there for the funeral?'

'No. That isn't necessary. The agent at Warby will see to everything.'

The children had stayed on at the Vincents' until the inquest was over but now they would be coming home. A female cousin had arrived to keep Decima company, and she had of course written to her brother, but had not heard from him yet.

Pamela was so embarrassed by the mere mention of George Fabian that she was unable to comment on this news.

Hubert's death—or the manner of it, so much more dramatic than his life—had cast a shadow over the neighbourhood. For the time being there were no invitations to dinners or picnics. One social event had to be attended: the Handel Festival at Aulingford Minster. This had been started half a century before to raise money for the charity school for orphan boys and girls founded by a pious Elizabethan lady of the Cressinder family. Naturally Richard and Pamela were among the patrons.

They drove to Aulingford on an oppressively hot, heavy afternoon and it was a pleasure to enter the great minster church which was deliciously cool and filled with soft, dusky light, after the painful glare outside.

They had to walk the whole length of the aisle to their places at the front and the pews were already filled with people they knew. Pamela was not sure how much she ought to bow and smile in such surroundings. They were in church, after all, but they were not going to a service, everyone was talking quite merrily, and she did not want to appear stiff and reserved, too much the great lady. Perhaps she went too far in the direction of friendliness, for she had the impression that people were looking at them a little askance and not responding to her smiles. She glanced

at Richard and saw that he was staring into the middle
distance and frowning, the scar dragging down the
corner of his eye. She hoped she had not annoyed
him again.

The band assembled in front of the choir stalls and
the proceedings began with an organ concerto, while
the choristers appeared in solemn procession, among
them many of the small orphans who had sweet treble
voices. Then they all settled down to perform the
chosen oratorio which this year was *Messiah*.

Richard said it generally was. There was a keen
musical set in Aulingford with a great liking for
Samson, *Solomon* and other works by Handel but
everyone else clamoured for *Messiah*. Pamela did not
mind. She loved the music which she knew well and
which seemed in a wonderful way to raise her spirits
and her confidence, both at a low ebb.

There was an interval halfway through which she
thought was a pity; she would rather have stayed under
the influence of Handel, instead of having to move
about and chat.

However she looked around her, prepared to be
agreeable, and was surprised to find that she and
Richard were practically isolated, everyone in the ad-
jacent pews having flocked out into the aisle.

Richard was still frowning. He said abruptly, 'I
want to talk to Howland.'

John Howland was a connection of the
Carriswoods and a particular friend of Richard's because he too had been a soldier. He was standing just
below the pulpit, and as they moved towards him
people separated to let them pass, which might have
been a sign of respect only it did not feel like that. It
felt as though they were being avoided. As though

everyone in the great church knew about the single bottle in Richard's dressing-case and believed he was a poisoner. That was ridiculous—as ridiculous as those Gothic fancies which had haunted Pamela when she first knew him and was frightened by his appearance and his ancient, overpowering house. A large community of sensible people would not suddenly decide that one of their most distinguished members had become a cold-blooded poisoner. Even the odd story of the dressing-case could not have become public property. It had not been mentioned at the inquest. She was becoming the victim of her own nerves.

John Howland at least was not avoiding them. He was talking in a low, urgent voice to Richard. Pamela felt she needed some air. There was a door in the north aisle leading to the cloisters. She stepped through it into the open arcade beyond. The building she had just left was the only part of the ancient monastery which remained intact because the townspeople had bought it from Henry VIII's commissioners and turned it into their parish church. All the rest had gradually decayed and the cloisters were a mere shell.

Standing on the covered pavement and looking across the churchyard, she was aware of several women who had passed through a gap in the wall on her right. She could hear without seeing them and she was pretty sure they could not see her.

'Everyone knows it was suicide,' a voice was saying. 'So why did they have to hedge the verdict?'

'To spare his children the stigma, and to give him the benefit of the doubt, I suppose. Only think, he couldn't have been buried in consecrated ground.'

It did not seem to strike the speakers that they themselves were enjoyably gossiping on consecrated ground as they discussed poor Hubert's death. Pamela identified the voices: Mrs Vincent, who had been Decima's hostess on the night of the fair, and an unmarried sister of Mr Carriswood.

There was also a Mrs Barber, who was known locally as a wit, and who said, 'I'm still not convinced that a man would kill himself because his wife refused to live in Yorkshire.'

Here there was some rather heartless laughter.

Miss Carriswood said, 'We ought not to treat the matter as a jest. It was her reason for refusing to go to Yorkshire that finally broke his spirit. In fact I think he only formed the plan of going there in order to get her away, once his eyes were finally opened to what was going on. They say everyone in London was talking about it.'

There was some whispering then, and Mrs Barber asked, 'Are you sure?'

Mary Vincent's voice rang through the fragile screen of the ruined cloister.

'Oh, yes, my dear: Not a doubt of it. You should have seen the way they behaved the morning he brought her the news of her husband's death. Coming all by himself to do so, I was never more shocked. Naturally I offered to go with her to Bourne House, I could hardly do less, but she wouldn't have me. She couldn't wait another moment to be alone with her lover.'

The words froze in Pamela's brain so that she hardly understood what was said next or who was saying it.

'. . . she must be completely besotted . . .'

'An experienced seducer, I hold him entirely to blame . . .'

'And his impudence in coming here to listen to sacred music...'

'Dragging that poor child along with him too. She looks scared to death, I'm sure he beats her...!'

'I dare say he does, my dear. There's bad blood in all the Cressinders.'

The voices moved away; the ladies must be going back into the church through a different door.

Pamela sat down on a stone ledge between the pillars. She felt stunned by what she had just heard. Not the confident assertion that Richard and Decima were lovers—she did not believe that any more than she had believed the rumour when Eliza Savage first told her of it in London. What appalled her was the suggestion that Hubert had killed himself because Richard had stolen his wife's affection. She realised that this might be true.

There was a step in the cloister and a shadow fell across the pavement. Richard stood beside her.

'I wondered what had happened to you. The music is about to begin. Are you not feeling well?'

'Just a little fagged from the heat.' She thought she must be looking ghastly.

'Would you like me to take you home?'

There was nothing she would have liked better when she thought of the congregation in the church, but if they left now everyone would say Richard had run away.

'No,' she said. 'We must stick it out.'

Richard muttered something she did not catch and slipped a steadying hand under her arm as they went back, literally to face the music.

Everyone else was already seated and it was unpleasantly public to be seen coming in late. She felt

a little better when the healing music began and she
was able to sit quietly, only half listening, and wondering if it could possibly be true that Hubert had
killed himself in an excess of jealousy and despair.
She had not seriously thought of suicide before, because it was such a dreadful and final act, not the sort
of thing you would associate with a devout churchman
like Hubert, domesticated, unimpassioned and having
on the surface no possible motive. It was a horrid
thought to admit, but she would have considered poor
Hubert too dull for such reckless and Byronic des-
peration. That was a trivial and shallow way to judge
another living creature. No one could say what agonies
he might have been suffering behind his somewhat
commonplace façade. He had been in much the same
situation as herself. How stupid not to have realised
that he might have disliked the friendship between
Richard and Decima as much as she did. She supposed that she, like the others, had taken him for
granted. In the violence of their lovemaking and
quarrelling, she herself had been able to challenge
Richard about his association with Decima and she
had trusted him to tell her the truth. She doubted
whether Hubert and Decima had ever discussed the
matter so frankly. So Hubert might have gone on
believing the worst, tried to get his wife away to another part of the country, and taken his failure as a
proof of everything he suspected.

The congregation rose to their feet, so she stood up
too, not knowing why until she realised they had
reached the 'Hallelujah Chorus' and were following
the precedent set by George II nearly a hundred years
ago. They were drawing towards the close and the
other great chorus. Now everyone was leaving.

Richard marched down the aisle, his head high, his mouth set, ignoring the people about him. Pamela did her best to follow suit, though being less than six feet tall it was not so easy for her to stare over lesser heads as he did. Their carriage was waiting. They were driven away.

As soon as the door was shut on them, he turned to her, saying, 'Those provincial dunderheads have all convinced each other that I was responsible for Hubert's death.'

'Is that what Major Howland told you?' she asked cautiously.

'More or less. I don't know how I'm supposed to have set about killing him, let alone why. Howland hinted and stammered and I was too angry to listen. In any case such accusations never have much to do with reason. Hubert died mysteriously and I am the obvious scapegoat. I thought the prejudice against our family had subsided. Apparently I was wrong.'

So he still did not know what was really being said about him. He thought he was being judged as a murderer, which naturally made him scornful and incredulous as well as angry. Her heart sank, for she felt she ought to tell him that he was really being condemned for something far less serious, though worse in a way, for it was very likely true.

And she couldn't get a word out. She was frightened of him because he had the power to hurt her so much. She remembered that woman talking in the churchyard, saying, 'She looks scared to death, I'm sure he beats her.' Richard had never beaten her. He simply cut her to the quick with cruel words.

They were well out of the town by now and crossing a bridge over the river Mallow. Richard tapped on the window and told the coachman to stop and put him down. 'You can drive her ladyship home. I'm going to walk. I need exercise.'

He would leave the road and go across country. She watched him stride off along the river bank, feeling bitter and persecuted, still not understanding why. What's wrong with me? she wondered. I used not to be such a miserable worm. She had been able to stand up and assert herself, before love and failure had destroyed her courage. The two men on the box were whispering to each other. No doubt they had picked up plenty of gossip in Aulingford.

She made up her mind, stopped the coachman just as he was preparing to drive on, and told him to wait. Then she too got out of the carriage.

She almost ran along the grassy bank, taking quick short steps in her narrow skirt. Her arms and shoulders felt clammy under the white muslin, for it was hotter than ever. The sky was now a sullen grey.

She caught sight of Richard standing on a small footbridge with his back to her and gazing into the river. He did not hear her coming until she was quite close and was taken by surprise.

'What are you running about for, in this heat? I told them to take you back in the carriage.'

'Yes, I know. But I thought I ought to warn you. To explain, that is. I don't think you perfectly understand what all those people are saying about Hubert's death.'

'And you do?'

'Yes, because I overheard Mrs Vincent and Miss Carriswood talking when they didn't think I was there. They think Hubert committed suicide.'

She was taken aback when he said, 'That's always been the most likely solution. The puzzle is, why? There doesn't seem to be an answer, so they've settled for murder instead.'

'They were suggesting that Hubert was unhappy because Decima didn't want to go to Yorkshire.'

Richard gave a derisive laugh. 'My dear Pam, you cannot seriously suggest that a man of Hubert's character would kill himself for such a reason as that?'

They were standing side by side on the bridge. She felt her palms sweating as she gripped the rail.

'He might have done so if he thought she wanted to stay here because she was in love with another man. With you.'

He did not explode into anger but was plainly exasperated. 'You've always clung to your unfounded suspicions about me and Decima. You must try not to credit everyone else with such fantasies.'

'They may be fantasies—in fact I'm sure they are— but they are not of my making. It was generally accepted in London two months ago that you were her lover.'

'I don't believe it,' he retorted furiously. 'But I can see you do. Who told you such a story? I suppose it was one of those sour-faced bitches who delight in making other women miserable.'

'It was Eliza. She told me by accident because she misunderstood something I said and thought I must have heard the rumours. When she found she was wrong she tried to withdraw, but of course she'd already said too much and I made her tell me the rest. She was quite overcome, poor Eliza. She assured me she and Hector knew it was all nonsense.'

'When was this? Back in June? Why didn't you let me know?'

She gazed ahead, not daring to look at him. Below their feet the river rippled in swirls of brown glass.

Then he said, in a different tone, 'You need not answer. You said nothing because you were afraid I should not listen, that I would simply say you were jealous. It must have been very disagreeable for you to know that such stories were going the rounds and uncommonly thoughtless of me to place you in such a situation. I'm sorry, Pam.'

She managed a sideways glance at him and saw that he was looking baffled.

'It doesn't signify, and I expect it was partly my own fault because I was not very friendly to Decima and I did not go with you to see her as often as you would have liked.'

'Well, I may be a poor sort of husband, but I'm not so churlish that I'm going to throw that in your teeth! I never saw any risk of scandal either, and I'm sure Decima didn't or she'd have told me to keep away. We enjoyed each other's company but we were never in the least in love.'

Decima was never in love with anyone but herself, thought Pamela, though she did not say so. She had at least learnt when to keep her mouth shut.

'And I still think it's outrageous,' he persisted, 'that she should be the victim of such malice. She's always been impeccably virtuous.'

'But that's the whole point.' Pamela was gaining courage at the sight of his bewilderment. 'In the circles we move in, it's hard to tell the unfaithful wives from the faithful. Outwardly we all conform. It's only the

Bel Fabians who ignore the rules and they are considered beyond the pale.'

'You are right,' he admitted. 'I should have been more careful of her reputation. I seem to have been abominably selfish towards you both.'

Astonished and defensive, he still hadn't grasped the full significance of what she had told him. It was not a question of whether he and Decima had or had not committed adultery, but whether Hubert thought they had.

A large cold bead of water splashed on Pamela's wrist. The sky was darker than ever. Richard collected himself.

'We're going to have a storm. What did you do with the carriage?'

'It's waiting for us on the road.'

'Come on, then.'

He took her hand and they raced along the bank, getting very wet in the process, for a heavy, drenching rain was now coming down in torrents. Pamela's elegant straw bonnet, put on for the Handel festival, flopped over her nose. They reached the carriage. He lifted her up and jumped in after her.

Once inside, he produced a large linen handkerchief and Pamela spent the short journey home trying to dry her neck and arms.

CHAPTER SEVENTEEN

BACK at Mallowdown, Pamela and Richard both went to change their wet clothes and then it was time once again to go in to dinner. Pamela was beginning to feel that her life consisted of endless uncomfortable meals. She supposed this was inevitable when two people led separate lives and only met when they had to. Though this time the awkwardness was different from anything that had gone before.

Confronting him down the long expanse of the dining-room table, she realised that Richard had now put recent events into their logical sequence and come to the same dreadful conclusion as herself. All the usual positive vitality had gone out of him, his face was rigid with shock.

In the presence of the servants it was impossible to talk about Hubert's death and it was clearly impossible for Richard to talk about anything else. Pamela felt obliged to chatter.

'I had a letter from Emily Everard, did I tell you? Lord Charles is back from France. You said he would be. Isn't that good? And they have engaged Mr Wyatt to make some alterations at Bradwyn. I have been wondering, Richard, do you think he could do some rooms for us here? There is the west wing, where no one ever goes because it is so dingy. I should like some nice tall rooms in the Gothic style, with fan vaulting and those pointed windows.'

Richard sat silent without any change of expression. She might have been talking Chinese. Thompson and the footman circulated with elephantine stolidity. She stopped talking and willed them to go away. Eventually they did.

Once they were alone, Richard got up and came to sit beside her, bringing the port decanter with him. He poured a glass each for them.

'I know you don't care for it, but it will do you good this evening. You need something to fortify you. I want you to tell me—do you think Hubert killed himself because he believed I was making love to his wife? Don't try to spare me.'

Pamela sipped the sweet heavy wine and made an effort to sort out her opinions.

'I don't see why we have to assume it was suicide. From what I know of Hubert it seems very unlikely to me.'

'Yes, but I'm afraid it is much the most convincing explanation of the facts.'

This shook her, and she asked, 'How do you make that out? At first you though he had been murdered.'

'I thought the circumstances very extraordinary. That's why I wouldn't let anyone touch the body. And it did seem possible that he might have been attacked by an intruder. Williams put paid to that. There were no outward signs of violence, though I was right in one respect: Hubert's death was not natural. But poison is not the weapon of a housebreaker caught in the act. Poison would have to be used by someone known to the victim acting with malice aforethought.'

She suppressed a shudder, and asked, 'Richard, where *did* that bottle come from? Was it out of your dressing-case? And, if so, how did it get to Bourne House?'

'I simply don't know. I've racked my brains and I haven't the faintest recollection of ever seeing it since I came home. We went to Brussels in such a hurry in 1815 that most of my stuff was left behind here. As a matter of fact I don't think the origin of the bottle matters as much as we thought it did at first, because I don't believe Hubert was murdered, or that he drank the laudanum by mistake for something else, which is the answer we should all prefer.'

'Why not?'

'Chiefly because of that cushion.'

'You mean the cushion that was under his head.'

'Yes. Think it out. If Hubert had swallowed the poison unknowingly, he would not have had the smallest foreboding that he was soon going to lose consciousness. When he began to feel drowsy and lethargic, he would most likely have sat down in one of the library chairs, passed into a coma and eventually died there, and that is where Beckley would have found him several hours later. On the other hand, the numbing sensation of the drug might have been so alarming that he would have made some attempt to revive himself, to fetch a glass of water perhaps, or go out into the fresh air. Once overcome by the narcotic he would have fallen, and a tall, heavy man, if he loses consciousness and falls from an upright position, generally staggers and flails about and ends in the most ungainly sprawl. He doesn't settle himself in a straight line with his arms folded under him and his head on a convenient cushion placed there for the purpose. There was no one else in the house to fetch the cushion or to arrange his limbs in a seemly position. I think he knew, the moment he lay down, what was going to happen.'

It all fitted in. There had been such a tidy look about that cushion. Pamela tried to imagine Hubert lying down on the floor for any more mundane reason and failed. He was far too formal a person. It did sound as though Richard was right.

He had been talking in a level, analytical voice. Now he suddenly leant on the table, propping his head on his arms and saying with a sort of groan, 'It is frightful to have brought such trouble on the Strangs. My oldest friends. What agony of mind he must have gone through before ending his life. And how deeply I have injured his children. I shall never forgive myself.'

'It wasn't all your fault. I don't want to say anything unkind, but after all Decima was married to him; surely she should have noticed if he was contemplating anything so dreadful.'

'We should both have noticed. Even so, I don't think she'd ever have guessed what was wrong. I don't think it often occurs to an innocent woman that she might be under suspicion. I was the one who should have foreseen the possibility. Heaven knows I've knocked around the world long enough.'

Pamela realised something she had never thought about. Richard had almost certainly come across jealous husbands before now. Why had he been so dense in this case?

He was already answering the question she had not asked.

'I never saw her in the same light as any of my former loves. I don't just mean because she was virtuous. Because she was different. I could spend a day in her company without any disturbing temptation.

My image of her was ideal, not romantic. I always admired her greatly, but admiration is not the same as love.'

'Of course not,' murmured Pamela.

No point in adding that they often looked very similar from the outside.

He must have realised this belatedly, for he said, 'I was a damned fool to let my feelings be so misconstrued. The truth is, I have thought of her for many years as the creator of a serene and happy home where life was ordered and pleasant and rational, and where there was all the charm and civilising grace of feminine society at its best. Totally unlike anything here at Mallowdown while my father was alive.'

Pamela had a flash of enlightenment. She remembered that Hector Savage had mystified Eliza by telling her that his friend Major Cressinder was not much used to the company of ladies. He had not meant that Richard was lacking in polish or poise, simply that he had not grown up in the sort of home that most men and women of their class took for granted.

At last she began to understand why he had fallen under the spell of Decima.

Richard began to talk about his father. She had tried to make him do so before but without success. Now he was quite explicit. After the death of his wife when Richard had been six, the late Lord Blaise, already a rake, had carried his drinking and his pursuit of women to such a pitch that he had no longer been acceptable in good society if ladies were going to be present, though he had kept up with his men friends in the hunting field or at his club. The women servants at Mallowdown had either become pregnant or had been hastily removed by their mothers. Lord

Blaise had installed a succession of mistresses, shrill, ignorant and predatory, most of them, whose manners had been worse than their morals and who had seldom lasted more than a month or so. His boon companions had been men who had overstepped the mark in one way or another. It had not been a suitable house in which to bring up small boys. His lordship had been a careless parent but he had sent them to Harrow as soon as he could. When they had come home for the holidays, he had called them a pair of damned encumbrances, and they had never known whether to expect a pat on the head or a clip on the ear.

'He must have been a horrible man!' said Pamela indignantly. She glanced up at his portrait behind Richard on the dining-room wall. He looked thoroughly dissolute, with a jeering mouth and bags under his eyes that the artist had faithfully reproduced. The eyes themselves had a spark in them she had sometimes seen in Richard's. 'Did you hate him very much?'

'I didn't hate him at all. What I hated was the way we had to live, not fitting in anywhere. And the uncertainty of his temper. Children like to know where they stand. You mustn't believe all the stories they tell about him. He drank, but drink never became his master, nor did gaming. And it wasn't his having mistresses that horrified the neighbours so, it was his parading them around Aulingford for the pleasure of putting Mrs Carriswood out of countenance.

'I think he was attached to me in his way. He bought me a commission as soon as I asked him, and I gather he spoke with pride of my being in the Army. When they brought me home from Waterloo in such a shocking state, he actually wept. I can forgive my father everything except his treatment of Tom.'

'Tom took after him, didn't he?'

'Yes and no.' Richard sat back in his chair, and in his strong, scarred face she traced qualities he had inherited from his disreputable father and put to better use—independence and the ability to survive. 'Tom was unlucky. Nothing went right for him. When he rode to hounds, his horse was sure to fall and break its knees. If he pretended not to care, everyone called him heedless or stupid. He was frightened of my father, which I never was. Of course his being the heir made it all worse. He took to the bottle to give himself Dutch courage and rapidly went to ruin. He was killed driving his curricle while he was drunk. As you know, my father died of an apoplexy six weeks later.

'The Strangs were both exceedingly kind to me, and it was Decima who persuaded me to stay down here and put my house in order. She said I ought to restore Mallowdown and the Cressinder family to the position they had occupied in my grandfather's time.'

And he would have done it, thought Pamela, if poor Papa, meaning everything for the best, hadn't jockeyed him into marrying me to compensate for the loss of Lady Emden's legacy.

She no longer blamed her father, so worried about his money troubles, and thinking that his pretty daughter, with her ancient lineage and her good health, would make an excellent wife for the new Lord Blaise. He had not understood—old people never did understand—that marriage was no longer a matter of families bargaining over accountable assets. Men and women nowadays had a right to look for the particular qualities which each desired in the other so that they could live together in a harmony which gave some substance to the claim that marriages were made in heaven.

Her marriage to Richard, she thought sadly, had so definitely been made on earth.

CHAPTER EIGHTEEN

THE night continued stormy. Pamela woke in the dark to hear the rain shattering against her window and a closer, domestic sound which disturbed her far more: a slow, regular tread in the next room. Richard was walking up and down, unable to sleep and haunted by his sense of responsibility for Hubert's death.

By morning the sky had cleared. A message came that there had been a good deal of flooding in the lower part of the village close to the river.

Richard hurried off to inspect the damage and see what needed to be done. Pamela was glad of this; it would give him something else to think about.

She too had been thinking hard, her head still full of the events of yesterday. She found she had changed her mind on one fundamental point. She could not believe that Hubert had committed suicide. Richard's rational arguments had convinced her, but Richard had been suffering from remorse. Suddenly made aware that their neighbours thought he was Decima's lover, he had accepted the likelihood that Hubert thought so too, and, because he was honest and not one to run away from unpleasant facts, he had forced himself to accept the logical conclusion.

But I'm not obliged to agree with him, thought Pamela. I'm sure there must be some other explanation. If only I could talk to someone who was at Bourne House on the day of Hubert's death.

She could not question Decima for a number of obvious reasons. That left the servants, and she could not go over there and question them either. Of all her unsuitable acts, this might appear more shocking than anything she had done before.

She was looking out of the window at the fresh, clean world after the rain and saw two white figures moving against the sparkling green. The babies were being taken for their morning airing. They went in strict order of precedence: Nurse would undoubtedly be carrying the heir, while Roly, the younger twin, was in the arms of his own particular nursemaid Peggy. The under-nursemaid would be upstairs getting on with the cleaning while they were out.

It occurred to Pamela that this junior nursemaid Ann had been in service at Bourne House and had a sister still there. She had come to Mallowdown at short notice after the twins were born, when the unexpected arrival of two babies at once had meant that another maid was needed. Decima, with her usual efficiency, had produced a suitable girl out of her own laundry. Pamela was afraid Ann had not been given much choice in the matter, but she was willing and cheerful and had become very fond of the twins.

Acting on impulse, as she so often did, Pamela went upstairs to the second floor and into the day nursery, where she found fifteen-year-old Ann busily washing the paintwork, which to the mistress of the house seemed unnecessarily clean already.

The girl scrambled to her feet and curtsied, saying shyly, 'The children are out in the garden, my lady.'

'Oh, dear, it must be later than I thought,' said Pamela easily. She sat down in a basket chair, adding, 'Go on with your work. Don't mind me.'

For a minute or two she watched Ann wiping a damp cloth along the skirting-board. Then she asked, 'Are you happy here?'

'Oh, yes, my lady.'

Ann looked absolutely petrified, probably thinking this was the prelude to some sort of trouble.

'Good. I know you do your work very well. Did you enjoy the fair?'

She herself had persuaded Nurse to let one of the girls go with the other servants, and, as Peggy, who was a Londoner, considered herself above such carryings-on, Ann had been the lucky one.

'Oh, yes, my lady, it was a grand show,' she declared, sitting back on her heels and pausing in her labours. 'Most of all the fireworks. And there was fairings and hot pies and dancing on the green.'

'I expect you saw your sister and some of your old friends.'

Ann agreed that she had met the party from Bourne House, but apparently they had not been in very good spirits, on account of being so anxious.

Anxious about what? wondered Pamela, pricking up her ears. Could something have happened already at Bourne House which had led to Hubert's death? She asked a question.

The answer she might have calculated for herself.

'They are all so scared of losing their places, my lady, when the family moves to Yorkshire.' Ann pondered briefly and then ventured, 'Do you think they'll still go, Mrs Strang and the children, after what's happened?

Pamela stared at her. She had been seized by an extraordinary idea. Was it possible that one of the servants might have poisoned Hubert in order to prevent his moving to Yorkshire and closing Bourne House? It sounded fantastic, but times had been uncertain since the end of the war, work was hard to come by. There might be someone desperate enough to go to any lengths to safeguard a good place.

'I'm sorry if I was wrong to ask, my lady,' said Ann, abashed by Pamela's silence.

'There was no harm in your asking, but I have no idea what Mrs Strang will do now.'

Except that she has never wanted to go to Yorkshire and they must all know it.

Pamela needed time to think this out. Ann was still talking, saying how dreadful it was about poor Mr Strang, such a kind gentleman and they were all so sorry. Pamela was only half listening until her attention was caught.

'. . . They say he must have been done to death by robbers, the same wicked robbers that carried off poor Betty, for she hasn't been seen since that very day and no one knows what's become of her.'

'Good gracious, is that girl still missing?' Pamela had forgotten about the errant second housemaid. 'You must not go filling your mind with such ideas, Ann. Mr Strang's death has nothing to do with Betty. She never came back from the fair.'

'She never went to the fair, my lady.'

'What? How do you know?'

Ann began to tell her. It was a complicated recital, starting with what she had heard from her sister at the fair itself, plus the daily gossip passing between the two important houses, as it always did, by means of estate workers, villagers, grooms delivering messages and so on.

Betty had fallen out with her sweetheart, one of the footmen, just before the wagon had been due to set out for Aulingford. Joe had been making eyes at Sue Brown, one of the dairymaids. Betty had burst into tears and run back into the house and no one had seen her since.

'Mrs Bower didn't know that,' said Pamela.

Ann sniffed. 'Mrs Bower went in the gig with Mr Beckley. Not in the wagon.'

Pamela could distinctly hear, inside her own head, her mother's voice saying, 'Never gossip with servants.' It was one of the many prohibitions set like a protective hedge around the conduct expected of a lady, and it mattered rather more than, Never go out without wearing gloves, and a great deal less than the most vital prohibition of all, Never allow a man to take liberties.

Once again breaking the rules, Pamela asked, 'Where does Betty come from, do you know? Is she a local girl?'

'Oh, yes, my lady. She's Farmer Jackman's daughter from Beddoes.'

'Then I expect she's gone home.'

'Oh, no, my lady. She's not been there either. She's vanished away.'

'How very strange. Well, I must not keep you from your work any longer.'

Pamela smiled as she got up and left the nursery, thinking furiously.

Betty had not gone to the fair because of a tiff with her young man. Suppose she had been so unhappy that she had rashly decided to leave her place for the same reason—surely she would have gone home. But according to Ann she was not at Beddoes either. So what had become of her? Once Hubert's family and his servants were on the road to Aulingford, there had been only two people left at Bourne House, himself and this housemaid. True, it was a large house and they could have gone through the whole day without meeting. But if Hubert had died in the library while Betty was innocently in the servants' quarters, why had she disappeared at all? It seemed an odd coincidence.

Pamela sent an order to the stables for Firefly, her favourite hack, to be saddled. She had decided to make some enquiries of her own. She would go to Beddoes and see the girl's family. It was not a very promising plan, because, according to Ann, Betty had not gone home. But some of this kitchen gossip might be wrong; Betty might be at her parents' house after all, and, if she was, Pamela meant to question her. She might easily have something to tell which had not been unearthed by the coroner. And if it was true that she had not gone home, her parents might at least know or guess where she was.

It took her more than half an hour to reach Beddoes, which was on the far side of the Strangs' estate. The house was old and weather-beaten, dwarfed by its own barn, and the land around here was light and poor. The Jackmans might be tenant farmers, superior to cottagers and day-labourers, but they were not growing rich and up-to-date like so many of the yeomanry. The farmyard was a sea of mud after the storm. Pamela saw a girl in pattens filling a pail at the well. The girl, who looked about twelve, fled into the house, and Pamela rode round to the front and found herself being observed by an anxious face at a downstairs window. She smiled and waited confidently for the front door to open. The face was removed from the window but nothing else happened.

After a short wait, she leant across and rapped on the door with the handle of her riding whip. It was awkward because there was a large, unpruned rosebush in the way, but she did not want to dismount while there was no one to take her horse. At last the door opened gingerly and the owner of the anxious face looked out.

'Good morning, Mrs Jackman,' said Pamela cheerfully.

She did not know any of the Jackmans but guessed who this must be. She also knew, from experience, that every soul within five miles would recognise her as Richard's wife.

'Good day to you, my lady,' said Mrs Jackman, flustered. 'Was your ladyship wanting anything? I can't ask you in, for we're all at sixes and sevens, the children sickening with I don't know what, and the chimney not drawing just as I'm ready to bake.'

'Oh, dear, I must not keep you, then. I just wanted a word with Betty.'

'Betty's not here!' exclaimed her mother. 'I don't know why your ladyship should think she was.'

'I heard she'd left her place and I thought she must have come home. Where can I find her, if you please?'

'She's gone away,' said Mrs Jackman, and now she sounded not flustered but hostile. 'Gone to her friends for I don't know how long. I can't tell you any more. Will that be all, my lady?'

The thin, worried woman stared up defiantly. Pamela wished she had dismounted. Up here on her side-saddle, she felt like a ruthless Norman Cressinder persecuting a Saxon. A child's wail came from the house. Mrs Jackman went back inside, firmly shutting the door.

Pamela sat gazing at the farmhouse for a few seconds, but after this rebuff there was nothing to do but ride away, puzzled and disappointed.

Why had Betty gone into hiding? Did she really know something about Hubert's death? And what good would that be if she could not be found?

As she rode round the farmyard, avoiding the worst of the mud, a new idea struck her. The unfortunate Betty was probably pregnant. This would account for her extreme distress when she caught her sweetheart making up to another girl, and also for her suddenly leaving her good place. It was far the most likely possibility. And all I've done, thought Pamela, is to upset that poor woman and waste half the morning. I've found out nothing more about Hubert, and Richard will go on feeling guilty.

Sunk in despondency, she rode along the farm lane between two deep cart-ruts, now filled with water like miniature streams. It was no good moping. She gave Firefly a touch of her heel and he broke into a canter.

She was coming to a bend in the road when a large, rough-looking man stepped out from behind a wayside oak and barred her passage. Firefly shied violently and Pamela nearly shot out of her saddle.

'What do you mean by frightening my horse?' she exclaimed, more annoyed than alarmed and fumbling with her foot for the stirrup.

'I beg your pardon, ma'am, I didn't mean to scare you. Might I ask what you want with my sister?'

'Your sister?'

She surveyed the young man who, though big and burly, had nothing really rough about him apart from his working clothes.

'You are Betty's brother?'

'Ralph Jackman, my lady. I overheard you talking to my mother. If you'd be pleased to tell me what it is you want with Bet, I might be able to help you.'

'You know where she is?'

He did not answer directly. 'She's gone to ground, fearing she may be blamed for the squire's death, poor silly lass, and they—my mother and father—haven't the heart to tell her that she ought to come forward and bear witness. But what I say is, she can't stay hid forever, and we need a bit of advice from someone who understands about the law. And when I saw you, I wondered if his lordship would tell us what Bet ought to do.'

Pamela's brain was beginning to go round in circles. 'Did you say that Betty is afraid of being blamed for Mr Strang's death? How did she come to be concerned? Do please tell me what happened.'

'I can't do that, my lady. It's for Betty to tell her own story. And I don't think she'll talk to you, indeed I wouldn't ask her to, unless you'll give me your word you won't turn her over to the magistrate.'

This was all said respectfully but with great firmness. Pamela realised that the girl was somewhere quite close—probably she had been in the farmhouse all the time—but she would not be allowed to see her unless she was prepared to give this promise. Yet how could she, when she did not know what Betty was going to reveal? Fantastic and improbably ideas about Hubert and a young housemaid ran through her distracted mind . . .

She was tempted to pretend she simply wanted to help Betty and would do what she was asked. But it would not be true. She only wanted to help Richard. How could she listen to some sort of confession, having sworn to keep quiet about it?

Then she saw a way out of this dilemma. The inquest was over, no one was in danger of being arrested, and Hubert himself had not been branded as a suicide. What Betty had to say might do more harm than good if it was made public. The really important thing was to clear Richard in the light of his own conscience, and perhaps this could be achieved without breaking any promises. The gossip, though unpleasant, did not matter so much.

'Your sister's secret will be safe with me,' she said, 'provided I can share it with my husband. You can have no objection to that and I hope you will tell her so. You said you would like to consult him.'

Ralph Jackman made no difficulties. It was lucky, she thought, that men always assumed that women needed a male adviser to confide in. Ralph said he would speak to his sister immediately, confirming Pamela's suspicion that she was lurking somewhere around the farm.

They returned towards Beddoes by the short cut which had taken him to the oak tree ahead of her, cutting across the corner of a cornfield which had been flattened by yesterday's storm.

Approaching the farmstead from behind, he asked her to dismount and showed her into the barn while he went off, presumably to fetch Betty.

Pamela sat down on a heap of straw to wait.

She was in a high state of nervous expectation. She could not imagine what Betty Jackman was going to tell her, or why she should have done anything that would bring her into danger from the law. Poor Hubert, always so respectable, surely there could not have been intrigues with maidservants under Decima's nose?

She had to wait a long time, and was reminded of that other occasion, in Harley Street, when she had sat kicking her heels while Bel Fabian abducted Alice. Here she was once again doing something outrageous, questioning one of Decima's servants behind her back, the sort of thing that made Richard angry and embarrassed and ashamed of her. No good will come of it, she thought gloomily. Perhaps nothing at all would come of it. The girl would refuse to meet her.

Then she heard light footsteps coming towards the barn and a rather plain young woman came in, pale-faced as though she had been ill but otherwise neat and collected.

'Oh, my lady!' she began. 'Ralph shouldn't have put you in here, it's not fitting. Only we didn't like to bring you into the house because my mother is in such a taking. I am so sorry to put your ladyship to this inconvenience.'

She had lost her country accent, like most superior servants. Pamela did not think she had ever seen her before, but she could picture her moving about, quiet and competent, in the high airy rooms at Bourne House.

'I don't at all mind the barn, Betty,' she said. 'Come and sit down.'

Betty hung back. Either she was afraid of seeming presumptuous or she did not care to sit in the straw. In the end she was persuaded to sit primly with her hands folded, a few feet away from Pamela, and to tell her story.

This began with her getting ready to go to the fair with the other servants and changing her mind at the last minute, though she did not at first give any reason. She had spent some time in the kitchen quarters and after a while ventured into the hall. Again she did not say why, though Pamela guessed that she had been sampling the novelty of walking about in the front of the house just as she pleased, as free as air. And all of a sudden she had heard a man's voice calling from the library.

'It was such a surprise, my lady, I didn't know what to do. My heart nearly jumped out of my mouth. I had thought to be quite alone in the house, I waited for a little and then I heard the voice again, and this time I knew it was the master and he was shouting, "Come and help me, whoever you are." I opened the library door and there he was, holding on to the table all doubled up like and as white as a sheet. He said, "Betty, is it you? I slipped on the library steps and I've wrenched my back."'

'He fell from the library steps?' said Pamela, frowning. 'That seems very odd. I was told there were no signs of injury, no bruises.'

'He didn't fall to the ground, my lady. The way he told it to me, he caught at one of the shelves to save himself, and twisted around as he was, he felt something go, like it might be a string breaking.'

I expect he tore a muscle, thought Pamela. She had heard this could be agonising, as painful as a fractured bone, especially if it was along the spine.

'I helped him to a chair,' continued Betty. 'Only he couldn't sit, he said it was worse than standing. He thought he might be better lying down, only none of the sofas were long enough. He was such a tall gentleman. And he didn't fancy trying to climb the stairs to his bed with only me to help him. So nothing would do but he must lie on the floor, and he said that wasn't too bad, so long as he turned on his chest with no weight to press against his back. He said he'd do well enough for an hour or two till the pain wore off and I was to give him a cushion from one of the chairs, which I did.'

'So that was why he had the cushion!' interrupted Pamela.

It had been the most difficult piece of evidence to account for, the most suggestive of suicide.

'He asked me to fetch the brandy from the dining-room and he drank a little, but he was still in great pain. So I went to see if there was anything I could give him out of the medicine chest. But when I got upstairs, I found it was locked—which I might have known it would be, if I'd stopped to think. And while I was searching my mind what to do for the best, it came to me that the little bottle of laudanum might still be on the shelf at the back of the wall cupboard in Madam's dressing-room. And, sure enough, it was.'

'Are you telling me that little glass bottle came out of Mrs Strang's dressing-room? Why didn't she say so?'

'I expect she's forgotten, my lady. It's a long time ago she put it there. Three years and more.'

'But what was it doing there? Why didn't she lock it up in the medicine chest?'

'I couldn't say, my lady. It wasn't my place to ask.'

'No, of course not. Go on.'

'I took the bottle down to the library and gave it to the master, hoping it might bring him some relief.'

Betty burst into tears. Through her choking sobs she blamed herself for having left the bottle with Hubert without explaining to him that it contained undiluted tincture of laudanum, far more lethal than the weak solution present in different types of physic when it was necessary to deaden pain.

Pamela was rather surprised that Betty had realised this if Hubert hadn't. Then she reflected that Hubert was a man who had never had anything wrong with him and was not used to dosing himself. He had been suffering acutely and impatient for any sort of relief. Why Decima had had a bottle of laudanum in her dressing-room was too complicated to think about now.

Betty, mopping her eyes, said, 'You haven't heard the worst of it. I went away and left him. He told me to go, and I said to myself I'd come back later to see how he did. I went up and lay down on my bed, and I fell asleep without meaning to. The next thing I knew, the stable clock was chiming seven. I must have been up there for six hours. I don't know how it happened—you'd think it was me had been at the brandy, though I swear I never touched a drop. It's true I'd hardly slept the night before, but all the same, who's going to believe such a tale?'

'I can for one,' said Pamela, remembering the story of the faithless footman. 'You had troubles of your own perhaps. Is that why you didn't go to the fair?'

'Yes, it was,' admitted Betty in a low voice. 'There was someone I thought liked me, and then I heard he'd been ogling that nasty Susan and he didn't deny it. Only none of those judges and justices is going to care about that, or see that it makes any difference to my sleeping all day and letting the master die. I can't make sense of it myself.'

'It is not nearly so strange as you think. People often sleep very heavily if they are unhappy. If they can sleep at all—and you were already worn out.'

She knew this because she had cried herself to sleep a good many times recently, and found some kind of escape, even though she had woken unrefreshed. In poor Betty's case the temporary escape had proved disastrous.

She persuaded the wretched girl to describe the final events of that dreadful day. How she had hurried downstairs, at first only concerned because she had left Mr Strang for so long. There had been a moment of relief when she had opened the library door and thought he was asleep, but as she approached him he looked so very odd that she had stood gazing in horror, not knowing what to do. Finally she had touched him cautiously and found he was already stiff. Close by him on floor had been the brandy glass, the decanter and the almost empty bottle of laudanum.

She had automatically picked up the glass and decanter and put them on the table. She did not remember what had happened to the bottle; she must have kicked it under the bureau. In her state of panic she could hardly remember anything else. She not only felt like a murderess but believed she would be accused of killing her master deliberately. She had run away because she was too terrified to stay where she was and try to explain. In fact she had lost her head completely.

And of course her flight had made everything seem worse. She knew she ought to come forward but she had been too frightened, and her parents were frightened too. Her mother was convinced she would be hanged, and, if her father had rather more common sense, he was afraid she would be put in prison and sent for trial, and that would be almost as bad as a death sentence to such a girl.

Only Ralph insisted that she ought to speak out, and that Mr Carriswood and those other gentlemen would accept her story and not put her in prison. What did her ladyship think?

'I think your brother is right,' said Pamela. 'I don't see why anyone should accuse you of committing such a horrible crime. In fact it would be a great comfort to everyone to learn that there never was a crime. Did you know that many people suspect Mr Strang of taking his own life?'

Betty was appalled. 'I shall have to tell, shan't I?' she faltered. 'For the sake of Madam and the poor little children.'

'I think that will be the best and bravest thing you can do, but first let me talk to Lord Blaise. He will see you are fairly treated and find a lawyer to speak for you if need be.'

Pamela was extremely sorry for Betty and promised to come and see her again soon. She had a brief conference with Ralph, who was only too grateful for her intervention. It was rather embarrassing to be thanked as a benefactress, when everything she had done had one end in view: to rescue Richard from his own mistaken sense of guilt.

As soon as she could escape from the Jackmans, she rode home at a neck-or-nothing pace, hardly able to think straight or consider the one puzzle that remained.

CHAPTER NINETEEN

THE first person Pamela met as she entered the hall was Richard.

'Where the devil have you been?' he demanded. 'They tell me you went out two hours ago without taking a groom. You ought to know better than to frighten us all like this.'

Pamela was too carried away to be intimidated. 'I'm sorry,' she said vaguely. 'I didn't mean to frighten anyone, but I haven't been wasting my time. I've got some news for you. I know how Hubert died. It was an accident—a horrid, unnecessary accident—but at least you haven't got his death on your conscience.'

He stared at her. 'What is all this? Who have you been talking to?'

'Can we go somewhere private?'

He took her into the walnut room off the hall, where the business of the estate was conducted and all the leases were kept. There was a circular rent-table with numbered drawers. He pushed her into a chair and stood looking down at her.

'What have you been up to, Pam?'

She told him everything. He listened without interruption, watching her as though he were reading her lips at the same time in order to be quite sure of what she said.

'I can scarcely believe it,' he said at last.

'I'm sure she was telling the truth.'

'Oh, yes, I don't doubt it. The Jackmans are a most respectable family and why would she lie? But I persuaded myself it was my fault.' His voice shook a little.

'Well, you need not think so any longer. Poor Hubert, if only he hadn't drunk so much of the laudanum—and the brandy. He was so careful as a rule.'

'That cuts both ways. He was the sort of man who thought, if one dose of physic is good, better be on the safe side and take two.'

'There was a perfectly good reason for his lying down with a cushion under his head but we should never have guessed it in a hundred years. And although the pain in his back must have been intolerable, I suppose such an injury would leave no sign after he was dead.'

Richard said slowly, 'I don't know how to thank you. You have shown so much more wit and perception than anyone else, gone to such extraordinary lengths—it is such a relief to know he did not kill himself. I'm eternally grateful.'

Pamela did not want to be thanked. It seemed to her only natural that a woman should support her husband in a crisis, no matter what terms they were on. And, although Richard spoke of his relief, he still looked anxious and unhappy. Was he too beginning to wonder why Decima had denied all knowledge of the bottle of laudanum?

As it turned out, he was thinking of something quite different, for he took her by surprise when he said, 'I've got enough on my conscience without Hubert's death. I know I've treated you very badly and I'm truly sorry.'

'You need not be. I never seriously believe you were Decima's lover.'

'I wasn't speaking of that. I should never have told you how our marriage was arranged. It was a dastardly thing to do, and the fact that we both lost our tempers is no excuse. Will you try to forgive me?'

'Of course.' She was acutely embarrassed. 'I mean, I have already—that is to say, there was no question of forgiving—it was better to tell the truth.'

Though she would have given almost anything not to have heard that particular truth.

He avoided her eye. His expression was bleak; they were separated by a great distance and were each searching for something to say when they were distracted by something that was happening outside the window.

A yellow post-chaise drawn by four horses had driven into the forecourt. Who in the world could this be? They both studied the carriage with a certain resentment. This was not the moment for welcoming uninvited guests.

A tall gentleman was stepping out. He had a military air about him and would have been handsome if he had not been so thin.

'I've never seen him before,' said Pamela. 'Have you?'

'It's George Fabian.'

'Oh.'

She flushed as a good many uncomfortable memories flooded back, but she could not help being intrigued. Colonel Fabian was offering his arm to another passenger.

'There's a lady with him. I wonder who—good gracious! Do you see who it is? Mary Jane Stevens. They must have come to fetch Alice.'

'We'd better go and meet them.'

They went out into the forecourt and met Colonel Fabian coming towards them, leaving heavily on a stick. Pamela had not realised he was lame. He hailed them with enthusiasm.

'My dear Richard, I apologise for this intrusion. Unexpected post-chaises are never a pleasant sight.'

'Always delighted to see you, my dear fellow.'

'I hope Lady Blaise is delighted too. How do you do, ma'am? I feel as though I know you already since you wrote me that very kind letter.'

Pamela took care not to look at Richard. She murmured something non-committal and turned to Mary Jane, who was still lagging unaccountably by the carriage. When Pamela smiled at her, she turned away. This was disconcerting. I suppose she blames me for deceiving her and getting her into that dreadful scrape with Decima, thought Pamela regretfully. It's no more than I deserve. But she found herself struck dumb.

'Come here, Mary Jane,' Colonel Fabian commanded. 'What are you doing skulking in the background? Lord and Lady Blaise are not going to eat you.'

'I should think not,' said Richard. 'How do you do, Miss Stevens?'

'That's the trouble,' said Fabian. 'She isn't Miss Stevens any longer and she thinks I ought to have told you so in advance. Allow me to present Mrs George Fabian.'

'Good heavens!' exclaimed Pamela, gazing from one to the other. 'You are married! I *do* wish you joy.'

'Are you sure you don't mind?' said Mary Jane, breaking into speech. Her eyes, though smiling, were still a little apprehensive. Pamela now realised she was wearing a very becoming green dress and an enormous straw bonnet, not at all governessy.

'Mind? Why ever should we? It is the best news I ever heard. You must tell me everything—have you come to fetch Alice?'

By this time they were entering the house. Once they were all seated in the summer parlour, Fabian gave a brisk account of what had been going on in Devonshire.

After dismissing Mary Jane, Decima had written her brother a detailed report of her disgraceful behaviour.

'Of which I didn't believe more than one word in twenty,' he commented placidly.

He had ridden over to call on Mary Jane at her father's parsonage, to assure her of his continued trust and to talk about Alice. One thing had led to another, he explained with a smile at his bride. They had decided to get married very quietly, break the news to Decima afterwards, and then reclaim his daughter. Pamela's letter had taken him by surprise; that was why he had written to Richard saying he meant to come and settle matters at Bourne House in about a month's time, though giving no reason for the delay. The marriage had gone ahead. George and Mary Jane had been in Weymouth on their wedding tour when they received the news of Hubert's death. It was now urgent that George should come to see his sister and of course he would have to tell her he was married, though he was afraid she would not be very pleased. That was why they had come to Mallowdown first.

Could Mary Jane stay here until the feelings of her new sister-in-law became clear?

Of course she could stay, said the Blaises in unison.

'I don't want to make an awkwardness for Mary Jane,' said Fabian, 'and though I think Decima has treated her abominably, she is my sister and I'd prefer not to quarrel with her just after she's lost her husband. But do tell us, if you please, what was the cause of Hubert's death? I couldn't make head or tail of Decima's letter. The whole business sounded most extraordinary.'

'So it was,' said Richard, 'and not the least extraordinary part is the fact that Pamela has this morning unearthed the explanation which defeated everyone else. She was in the middle of telling me all about it when you arrived.'

Of course she had to tell it all over again, with occasional interpolations from Richard and questions from Fabian. When she came to the little bottle that contained the laudanum, he asked,

'What was it like?'

'It seems to have come out of my dressing-case,' said Richard. 'Part of a matching set. And the odd thing is I simply cannot recall giving it either to Decima or Hubert, though clearly I must have done so. I'm sure there was never any laudanum in it. Unless I've altogether lost my memory.'

There was still a trace of anxiety in his voice.

'Calm yourself, Richard,' said Fabian. 'You were not the only young cavalry officer who set out for Spain armed with all the most expensive camp furniture that Bond Street could provide. I had one of those dressing-cases too. Did you never think of that?'

'Good heavens—it never entered my head. And the bottles were identical. Well, of course they would be if they came from the same shop. That's a relief anyway. I don't know which I disliked most, the general suspicion that I was a liar or my own private suspicion that I was losing my wits. And all the time it was you who gave the bottle to Decima.'

'I did not give it her,' said Fabian with a curious deliberation. 'She took it away from me.'

'Took it away? Whatever for?'

'Do you mean to say she never told you? Well, if that isn't Decima all over! I can understand her not wanting to let the whole world know of my unfortunate weakness, but to keep it a secret from such an old friend! That's always been her trouble, hasn't it? Anyone connected with her has to come up to her own exalted standards.'

George Fabian had flushed. Mary Jane reached out a hand and clasped his wrist, as though to offer some kind of strength. Pamela, mystified, knew they were on the verge of some kind of revelation but could not imagine what.

Richard was quicker and more experienced. 'You were taking laudanum? No, I never knew. You have my sympathy. It's a devilish form of servitude.'

'He's over it now,' said Mary Jane. 'He cured himself by his own strength of will, which is more than most men could have done.'

'I was obliged to be back to Devonshire and live like a hermit before I could do it,' said her husband. 'So long as my dear sister was moralising over me and treating me like a child, I grew steadily worse. I used to bribe her servants to buy the stuff for me from the apothecary in Aulingford. They were threatened with instant dismissal if they were caught supplying me with the juice of the wicked poppy. I wasted a great deal of ingenuity in finding new hiding-places for it, but I seldom succeeded in outwitting her.'

He laughed uncertainly and Richard regarded him with compassion.

'You must have had a wretched time. What did Hubert have to say about all this?'

'Not very much. He hardly ever dared voice an opinion, poor old Hubert. Though I do remember his once suggesting that I should break myself of the habit little by little. And Decima replied in her loftiest manner that giving in to temptation was always wrong, and that she must deprive me of the means of destroying myself, however much it hurt her to do so.'

Richard drew a sharp breath. Pamela glanced sideways at him, but he had turned a little sideways in his chair and she could not see his face.

George Fabian said, 'I interrupted you, Lady Blaise. Do go on telling us about Hubert.'

Pamela described the whole sequence of events as best she could, this time with no help from Richard, who sat leaning on the table, deep in thought.

'A tragic business,' said Fabian at last. 'Though it's a great deal better than suicide. I imagine the brandy went to his head—he drank so little as a rule—and in a confused and reckless state of mind he swallowed off the laudanum to be rid of the pain.'

'If only he'd understood how dangerous it was,' said Pamela.

'He wouldn't,' said Mary Jane. 'He took very little interest in his health. If he ever had anything wrong with him, he simply drank the physic Mrs Strang gave him without asking what it was.'

He really would have been an extremely easy person to murder, thought Pamela. Anyone could have done it. Was that why Decima had pretended not to recognise the little glass bottle with its tell-tale dregs of laudanum? Because she was afraid of being accused of killing her husband?

Abruptly she asked, 'Why didn't she throw it away? Not the bottle itself. The laudanum.'

'I dare say it was an oversight,' said Fabian prosaically. 'Though she won't care to admit that. She's never at fault, haven't you noticed?'

Richard gave Pamela a fleeting glance and looked away again.

They had been talking so earnestly that they had not heard the sound of a new arrival. Suddenly Thompson appeared in the doorway, looking conspiratorial.

'Mrs Strang's carriage has just driven up, my lady. Am I to show her in here?'

'Oh. Yes. That is, I don't know,' began Pamela doubtfully.

'Talk of the devil,' muttered Fabian.

'I'll have a word with her first.'

Richard got up, unconsciously squaring his shoulders as though to face an unpleasant task in a military manner, for he could no longer have any doubt that Decima knew where the laudanum had come from.

After a moment's hesitation, George followed him out of the room.

The two women were left alone.

'What is she doing here?' Pamela wondered aloud. 'She hasn't left the grounds of Bourne House since Hubert died.'

In fact there was a simple explanation though they did not hear it until later. Colonel Fabian and Mary Jane had been seen together in Aulingford by one of the Bourne House grooms who had ridden in to fetch the post. He had reported to his mistress, who had come to consult Richard.

So she could not have been entirely unprepared for her brother's news, and, when the door opened again after a fairly short interval, Pamela could hear that her old enemy was fully in command of the situation.

'Of course I intend to see her, George.' The cool voice floated in ahead. 'I dare say she is afraid of meeting me, and I don't wonder at it. She should have thought of that before she married you.'

Mary Jane threw an agonised glance at Pamela, who gave her an encouraging smile, saying, 'She cannot hurt you now. Colonel Fabian won't let her.'

Decima made her entrance. Her colour was heightened and this, with the severe black of her mourning, was rather becoming. Pamela and Mary Jane rose to greet her. Barely acknowledging her hostess, Decima addressed her new sister-in-law.

'May I congratulate you, Mrs Fabian? You have certainly worked hard enough to achieve your object and that must be a satisfaction to you. I hardly know whether to wish you joy. It must be clear by this time that my brother is not very skilful in his choice of wives. He seems to rush from one extreme to the other.'

Wisely, Mary Jane made no attempt to answer back or to defend herself. She behaved with great dignity, merely saying, 'I knew you would not like our news, ma'am, and I only wish you had not heard it at such a sad time. Please allow me to say how sorry I am for your great loss. Mr Strang was so truly good and kind.'

Decima was temporarily disarmed. She looked bereft and forlorn, as though she had only just remembered how different her life was going to be without Hubert always in the background, cherishing and devoted, sharing her troubles and admiring her triumphs. Then she remembered a minor grievance.

'I think you might have got here a little sooner,' she said to her brother.

'We came directly we received the news. Your letter followed us to Weymouth. It is a sad business but at least there is no longer any question of suicide.'

'Suicide!' repeated Decima. 'What can you be thinking of, George? No one would suspect Hubert of doing anything so wicked and irreligious, even if he had a reason, which he most certainly did not.'

They did not contradict her, though Pamela and the Fabians kept quiet more out of consideration for Richard than for Hubert's widow.

Richard said, 'You owe it to Pamela that we now know the truth.'

He gave her a brief account of what had happened at the Jackmans' farm.

Pamela had half expected that Decima would be overcome by astonishment and chagrin. She should have known better.

'So it was all the fault of that stupid girl!' was her first comment. 'I guessed that Hubert must have suffered some indisposition or minor accident, though naturally I hardly imagined a fall from the library steps. But he would never had thought of dosing himself with laudanum on his own initiative. Poor Hubert, he would be alive today but for Betty

Jackman's interference. She killed him and I hope she is properly aware of it.'

Pamela opened her mouth to speak, but for once in her life mastered her indignation.

It was Richard who said, quite gently, 'You must regret leaving such a dangerous drug where she was able to find it.'

For an instant it seemed as though Decima might break down and agree with him. Then she said sharply, 'Betty had no business to go looking in my cupboard. It was very wrong of her. She knows it, too, or why else did she run away? If I had been there——'

'But you weren't there,' Richard pointed out. 'You were not expected back until next day. I suppose the poor girl felt she had to do something. It was a sequence of unlucky accidents. What I can't understand is, why you lied to Carriswood afterwards. In the shock of Hubert's death you may have forgotten about the laudanum. Once you were shown the cut glass bottle, I am certain you remembered everything about it. Why didn't you tell the truth?'

He spoke very quietly, though by now the iron had entered his voice. He had not mentioned what he himself had gone through as a result of her silence. It was probably her attack on the well-meaning housemaid, her total refusal to accept any of the blame, which had disillusioned him.

She gazed back at him, her blue eyes limpid, her conscience apparently untroubled.

'There was no point in my revealing unnecessary details. It would have meant revealing private matters I don't wish to discuss. And all to no purpose. Knowing where the laudanum came from would not have brought Hubert back to life.'

Which was perfectly true.

Pamela listened with something like disbelief. She could have forgiven Decima for keeping quiet about the laudanum because she was frightened. Afraid she might be accused of murdering her husband. But of course that was ridiculous. It would simply never occur to Decima that such a dreadful charge could be brought against *her*. Any more than she could have imagined what was being said about her relations with Richard. Shut up in the seclusion of a newly made widow, she had not heard any of the rumours. She had kept quiet about the little glass bottle because she did not want to admit that a brother of hers had once been the slave of a disreputable vice. Or, worse still, that she herself had carelessly kept a lethal quantity of laudanum in an unlocked cupboard.

CHAPTER TWENTY

'SHE is entirely heartless,' declared Pamela. 'I don't mean deliberately cruel—I dare say it is not often deliberate. I mean unfeeling. There is something missing where her heart and her affections ought to be. I really believe she in incapable of caring for anyone but herself. Do you think she knows it?'

'No,' said Mary Jane. 'Women like her always consider themselves to be models of tenderness and devotion. It is their undeserving friends and families who turn out such a disappointment.'

Pamela laughed. 'I expect you are right. Don't let's talk of her any more. I want to hear about you.'

Decima had left, her self-consequence not at all diminished. George had arranged that he should follow her over to Bourne House to fetch Alice, and Richard had accompanied him to the stables. Pamela and Mary Jane were in the bedchamber which had been prepared for the guests, very grand and old-fashioned with its top-heavy canopy over the bed and dappled marquetry furniture.

'Dear Lady Blaise, it's hard to know where to begin.'

'You can begin by calling me Pamela. Thank goodness we don't have to keep our distance any longer. And you can go on to tell me what I most want to know: were you already in love with Colonel Fabian when I first knew you?'

'I'm afraid so,' admitted Mary Jane. 'Right from the start, though at the time he was a married man with a beautiful wife and they were my employers. Shockingly indelicate, wasn't it? I dread to think what my father would have said, had he guessed. It was just a hopeless dream, you understand. George wasn't aware of it. Hardly knew I existed. He had come back from Spain a desperately sick man, one side of his body shot to pieces. That was why he'd started on the laudanum. Lady Bel had brought him down to Aldercombe and he was beginning to recover.

'She engaged me to look after Alice, who was only five, rather young to need a governess. I think she wanted another person in the house, someone who was just that degree above the rank of a servant, whose presence would prevent her husband saying the things she did not want to hear. He had already found out what she had been doing while he was away at the war, and she knew he was too great a gentleman to humiliate her in front of the governess.'

'You cannot have been aware of all this at the time.'

'Oh, no, I was far too innocent. I only knew that they were unhappy and something was wrong. I worshipped him from afar and blamed her for being frivolous and bored. Then this man, her former lover, came to stay. George caught them together in the summer-house. I think he would have killed them both, only in his rage he forgot he was not so agile as he used to be. He slipped and fell, and reopened his old wound. While he was lying helpless in bed, his charming wife ran away.'

'She would!' said Pamela bitterly. 'I can imagine.'

'Well, to be fair, she must have known he would never live with her again. The worst of it was, his pain and distress combined to drive him back to the comforts of laudanum, just when he was managing to do without it. Decima came down to Aldercombe and insisted on taking us all back to Bourne House with her. I do believe she meant it for the best and George was in no condition to refuse. But she was the worst person for him to be with. You heard what he said about her spying on him and moralising. She was genuinely ashamed that any member of her family should be addicted to such a degrading habit. She hated my knowing, which I did, of course, and went to endless lengths to prevent the servants finding out; so ridiculous, when several of them were buying laudanum for him in the town.'

'Considering he'd been wounded fighting for his country, I don't see what there was to be ashamed of. He deserved pity and forbearance.'

'I believe Mr Strang told her as much once, but it didn't have much effect. She said he didn't understand her high ideals. After a few months George announced he was returning to Aldercombe. Decima hardly tried to stop him, but she insisted that Alice should remain at Bourne House. George agreed without a struggle and I was desolate; I could not bear to think of the state he might sink into in that great place alone. He has told me since that he was already becoming attached to me and hoped to marry me once he was divorced, but that he knew he must not marry anyone, or have Alice living at home with him, until he was free of that deadly drug.

'He went down to Aldercombe determined to cure himself and in the end he did. He put himself on a period of probation to make sure the cure was complete, and he was going to send for Alice and me in the autumn. He was wondering whether it would be scandalous for him to make me an offer of marriage while I was living in his house, and then, out of the blue, he heard from Decima that I had been sent away for intriguing with his former wife so that she could carry off Alice to France. Well, he didn't believe a word of that. He knew what I thought of Bel; not her moral failings, which are not for me to judge, but her selfish irresponsibility as a mother. And he guessed how I must be feeling. Indeed I was sunk in wretchedness and wondering whether I dared approach him and try to explain. He came to see me four days after I got home and everything was settled between us in a matter of weeks. Pamela, I never thought I could be so happy!'

'You deserve to be, after all you have gone through,' said Pamela warmly. 'It's like a fairy story.'

She would have asked a great many more questions, only then the door burst open and Alice almost flew into the room and flung herself on Mary Jane.

'Dearest Stevie, how glad I am to see you again! And Papa says we are all going to live at Aldercombe and you are going to be my mama. It is better than anything I ever dreamed of!'

No hankering after her real mother, Pamela noted with satisfaction.

Mary Jane kissed the little girl, who was thoroughly over-excited, jumping about on the edge of the stately bed, her cheeks flushed and her eyes sparkling. You could hardly recognise the pale, withdrawn child who had always behaved like a wax doll in the presence of her aunt. She actually looks like Bel, thought Pamela with a twinge of dismay. Would she grow up to resemble that wild, erratic beauty? But no. She had the loving heart which Bel and Decima both lacked, though its absence had affected them so differently. Mary Jane would be the right person to make the best of Alice. She was smiling now and trying to calm her down.

'You have not been at all polite to Lady Blaise, my love, rushing in here like a mad thing.'

'Oh, Lady Blaise, I am so very sorry,' said Alice with a beaming smile. 'How do you do? How are the darling twins?'

'They are growing into great hulking prizefighters. Would you like to go and see them?'

'Yes, I should, very much—if you don't mind, *Mama*.' Alice giggled over this first acknowledgement of Mary Jane's new status.

'Nurse will have a soothing effect on her spirits,' Pamela remarked, when Alice had gone off to see the babies. 'She keeps us all in order, even Richard.'

She wondered how long it would be before there was a nursery at Aldercombe.

The Blaises and the Fabians dined in festive style. To start with Pamela was afraid that Decima might be present as Banquo's ghost, but George soon got rid of her.

'I have a piece of interesting news for you all,' he announced. 'Decima is removing to Yorkshire.'

They stared at him in amazement.

'But why?' demanded Richard. 'She was dead set against the idea. She wouldn't go there while Hubert was alive, so why should she change her mind now?'

'That's just it. I pointed out that it was generally believed in the neighbourhood that Hubert had killed himself because she wouldn't go with him to Yorkshire.'

'George, you didn't?' exclaimed Mary Jane in a wifely voice.

The servants were removing the soup plates, their faces impassive.

'Certainly I did. Of course I added that the suicide story will fade out once Betty Jackman's evidence is known. I reminded Decima, however, that this would not greatly enhance her reputation when it is realised that she lied to old Carriswood and the coroner. And that she will still be criticised for refusing to go to Yorkshire. So now, believe it or not, she is ready to pretend that the story of their disagreement was just another malicious rumour and that she is departing for the North of England because it is what Hubert would have wished. And, what's more, she'll believe it herself by the time she gets there. There's nothing like hypocrisy for turning the brain. It's better than laudanum any day.'

Pamela felt a surge of relief. A hostile and self-righteous Decima only three miles away would have cast an ominous gloom over their lives, besides causing awkwardness and speculation among their neighbours. Now she would go away and leave them in peace.

That was something to be thankful for, and perhaps it was the only thing, for Pamela was beginning to take stock of her marriage as it stood, even without the complication of Decima.

Delightful as it was to see the Fabians so blissfully and romantically in love, their lively exchanges and glowing glances did draw a painful attention to the coldness which existed between her and Richard. And she knew now that this coldness was not just the result of their quarrels over Decima. He had never wanted the match. A mistaken chivalry had forced him into marrying her because her father had pointed out that, when he inherited Lady Emden's money, he had cut out Pamela who was going to be left penniless and would have to go for a governess.

Mary Jane, a genuine governess, had ended by marrying for love. Pamela did not for an instant grudge her that great reward, but it was ironic all the same. Not that she could ever have been Mary Jane's equal. She remembered Richard hinting acidly that she wouldn't have lasted long in that profession—governesses were not allowed to make mistakes. Wives, by implication, had to be endured, even when they made nothing else.

She glanced towards the end of the table. He was standing to carve a saddle of lamb, a skilled occupation which gave him an excuse to look serious and ignore the talk and banter of the others. She felt an aching love for him and a longing for his eyes to light up and his voice to lift with laughter, and for the intense passionate pleasure of that brief time in London when she had innocently imagined they were both in love. She was fairly certain everything would go better now Decima was out of the way, yet she could not help drawing a sad comparison between their calculated partnership and the Fabians', which did seem to be a real marriage made in heaven.

When dinner was over, Pamela took Mary Jane into the drawing-room, where the men followed them after the shortest possible interval spent drinking their port. Presumably George could not bear to be separated from his bride.

They sat around talking for a while, the Fabians surreptitiously glancing at the clock and George insisting that Mary Jane was tired after her long drive. Pamela had never seen a less weary-looking traveller.

It was ridiculous. George Fabian was a man whose sufferings had aged him considerably, he was the divorced husband of a notorious beauty who had made him a laughing-stock, he had now married his daughter's governess, a sedate young woman from a country parsonage. Yet they were so enclosed in their honeymoon atmosphere that Pamela, not yet nineteen, felt quite motherly towards them. In spite of everything she saw the funny side of this.

She looked across at Richard, who was becoming more and more silent. He stopped brooding for a moment and caught her eye with a gleam of amusement, before getting to his feet and ringing the bell.

'I don't know how it is,' he said casually, 'but I am uncommonly thirsty this evening. We need not wait any longer for the tea-table.'

Once the ritual of tea-making and drinking had been gone through, it was possible for Pamela to escort Mary Jane to her room.

When she came back again the drawing-room was empty. She supposed the men had gone for a final stroll before George Fabian joined his bride.

The formal upstairs drawing-room was not much used. The chairs they had been sitting in were all askew, pushed out of their regular positions. Flowery china teacups were balanced on tables and ledges, one of them half full of lukewarm tea. These small signs of occupation seemed almost slovenly in such a grandiose room. Pamela caught sight of herself in a long pier glass, slim and straight in a dress of yellow gauze, her strangely bright hair, the colour of pale copper, gleaming in the light of the chandelier.

You ought to be able to make a man love you, she thought. You're quite as pretty as Mary Jane. Or Decima, come to that. Or Emily Everard or Eliza Savage. She added to the list, thinking of the married women she knew best. In fact you're as pretty as almost anyone except Bel. If she followed Bel's example she would find plenty of men ready to love her. That was how many women in her world behaved, though most of them did so very discreetly, without running away and causing public scandals. She could never enter into such a liaison, not simply because it would be wrong, but because it would be utterly pointless. There was only one man whose love she wanted, and if she couldn't have that she would have to do without.

'What a fool you are to mind so much,' she said aloud to her reflection.

A voice behind her said, 'My darling, don't look so unhappy. What is it you mind?'

Richard had come in very quietly. She saw him now in the glass as he moved towards her, splendidly tall and dark, the light on the fine, regular side of his face, the scarred profile in shadow.

'Come and sit down,' he said, laying a cool hand on her arm and drawing her toward one of the large settees.

'I know I've made you miserable,' he said, 'by being so obstinate and prejudiced. You were right and I was wrong. I was completely taken in. Because I saw only her good points, I could not think what it was you found in Decima to dislike and resent; that cold, calculating vanity which I never dreamed of until today.

I have been as blind to her faults as she is herself. I could not have been more unreasonable if I had been in love.'

That was what Pamela had thought once, before she had realised how Richard saw Decima: as a symbol of that civilising grace and serenity he had never known at home.

Decima as a person had ceased to be a threat, and as soon as that had happened she had lost her importance. Now they were simply faced with the problem that had made her important. The fact that they would never have chosen to marry each other in the first place.

Richard was still looking stricken.

She said awkwardly, 'You mustn't blame yourself. She was a very old friend, and I haven't been much help to you, in the way of making improvements and so forth.'

She gazed rather hopelessly round the drawing-room. The wall hangings were a deep maroon and William Kent's heavily carved furniture had enough gold leaf on it to finance a bank. A French ormolu clock was sending out a chilly chime which seemed to shiver through the icicle drops of the chandelier.

'Are you proposing to improve this room?' enquired Richard, recovering a touch of sardonic amusement.

'Would you like me to try?'

'No,' he said so definitely that she felt snubbed.

Until he added, 'I prefer your other plan. These old rooms don't lend themselves to change and perhaps we ought not to spoil them. I think we should do better to keep them for grand occasions and pass our everyday lives in the west wing, after Wyatt has done it up for us, as you suggested.'

'I didn't know you were listening.'

'Well, I was and I thought it a very good notion. I tell you what, Pam: as soon as the weather is a little cooler we'll go down to Bath, rent a house there and take the twins with us. It is too bad that your mother has never yet seen her grandsons, and she will not leave your father to come to us. If we left the nursery contingent in Bath you and I could take a trip to Italy while the west wing is being made ready for us. How would that suit you?'

'Very well indeed.'

She spoke with real pleasure, for she knew he was anxious to make up for the past, and life still had a good deal to offer even if it was only second best.

Then he somehow spoilt everything by saying, 'I do love you so.'

'Oh, don't say that!' she burst out.

'I'm sorry,' he said in a mortified voice. 'Do you dislike me so much that you cannot endure any mention of love?'

'Of course I don't dislike you. I only want you to be honest with me, not to talk a lot of sentimental stuff that you don't mean, just to be obliging.'

'Obliging!' he echoed, his dark brows ominous. 'What the devil do you mean by that?'

'Perhaps it was the wrong word. Just to be kind, then. For I know what you really feel about me and why you married me. You told me, the day you learnt of my writing to George Fabian.'

'Oh, my darling, you don't still believe the horrible things I said to you then? I was an absolute brute, I was trying to hurt you. Don't hold that against me.'

'I know you lost your temper,' she said slowly, 'and I don't blame you. But if that was all, why have you been so set against me ever since, freezing me with your displeasure?'

'I freezing you! It was the other way round. I thought you had come to hate me and everything to do with our marriage. I was afraid to come near you.'

She gazed at him, uncomprehending.

'Perhaps you've forgotten,' he said, 'how that scene ended. At one point you said you had never wanted to marry me, which was certainly true, that it was all my fault the marriage ever took place, and then at the end you walked out of the room and never really spoke another warm word to me until the trouble over Hubert's death.'

Pamela was speechless. Though she had spent so long trying to interpret other people's feelings by what they said and did, it had never before dawned on her that her own attitude could be just as misleading.

She reached out a hand to Richard—he saw the bewildered entreaty in her eyes and made a grab at her. Then they were in each other's arms, laughing and kissing and crying. At least she was crying and she thought he was very near it.

After the kissing had gone on for some time, she managed to break away for long enough to ask a question.

'Surely you must have known I'd fallen in love with you during those early weeks in London? You cannot have forgotten how happy we were then?'

'I was afraid that might have been just a flash in the pan. Passion doesn't always lead to lasting love. I thought I'd spoilt everything.'

'I was sure I'd spoilt everything for you. You were so angry when you brought me down from London, and when I franked my letter to George Fabian by copying your signature, that was the final straw. You told me I could be hanged for forgery.'

'Did I really say that? What a pompous idiot I must have sounded!'

He gazed at her in horror and then they both began to laugh.

'Though it is no laughing matter,' he protested. 'A shocking thing for a man to say to his wife. Are you certain you can still love me, my precious girl?'

'Yes, Richard,' she whispered, melting into his arms.

Nothing could be easier than the love that had once seemed so impossible.

The other exciting

MASQUERADE
Historical

available this month is:

A PROUD ALLIANCE
Marion Carr

When the Honourable Felicity Travers discovered that her late father had arranged a marriage for her, she considered this stretched duty a little too far. For one thing, it was with Jarle Blakely, the man Felicity was convinced was responsible for her father's bankruptcy, and, secondly, inspired by the suffragette movement, Felicity intended to be a modern woman and make her own decisions.

But the entrepreneurial Blakely proved persuasive, if lacking in romance, and Felicity changed her mind. But there were secrets to unravel which led to nasty surprises, and until all was solved, their marriage surely had no hope of success?

ISABELLA
Janet Grace

Things were going drastically wrong for Isabella! Deprived of her poetical beau, and a season in town under her aunt's aegis, she was mortified to discover she was expected to accompany her young brothers to their tutor's home in the country. The next blow fell when her father announced her betrothal to the elderly roué, Lord Carton Crue.

Beseiged on all sides, Isabella wasn't best pleased to discover the tutor was no longer Me D'Estine, but had become Anthony, Viscount Alladay, heir to an earldom! Reviewing her life, and her perception of Anthony, Isabella's resolve strengthened – she *wouldn't* be a victim.

A PASSING FANCY
Deborah Miles

For the sake of his health, Cleo Montague and her father embarked from Plymouth for warmer climes. But the journey to Australia in 1858 proved too much for his strength, and Cleo found herself travelling on alone. Determined not to abandon her father's dream, and with superb millinery skills to earn her living, Cleo found herself setting up business in the goldrush town of Nugget Gully.

But this was only possible at the cost of accepting Jacob Raines as a silent partner. A decent respectable woman, Cleo knew that any hint about black sheep Jake would ruin her reputation in the community . . .

TWO HISTORICAL ROMANCES

& TWO FREE GIFTS!

NO STAMP REQUIRED

Experience the thrill of 2 Masquerade Historical Romances Absolutely Free!

*Experience the passions of bygone days
in 2 gripping Masquerade Romances - absolutely free!
Enjoy these tales of tempestuous love from
the illustrious past.
Then, if you wish, look forward to a regular supply of
Masquerade, delivered to your door!
Turn the page for details of 2 extra FREE gifts,
and how to apply.*

An irresistible offer for you

Here at Reader Service we would love you to become a regular reader of Masquerade. And to welcome you, we'd like you to have two books, a cuddly teddy and a MYSTERY GIFT - ABSOLUTELY FREE and without obligation.

Then, every two months you could look forward to receiving 4 more brand-new Masquerade Romances for just £1.75 each, delivered to your door, postage and packing is free. Plus our free newsletter featuring competitions, author news, special offers offering some great prizes, and lots more!

This invitation comes with no strings attached. You can cancel or suspend your subscription at any time, and still keep your free books and gifts.

Its so easy. Send no money now. Simply fill in the coupon below at once and post it to - Reader Service, FREEPOST, PO Box 236, Croydon, Surrey CR9 9EL.

— NO STAMP REQUIRED —

Yes! Please rush me my 2 Free Masquerade Romances and 2 Free Gifts! Please also reserve me a Reader Service Subscription. If I decide to subscribe, I can look forward to receiving 4 brand new Masquerade Romances every two months for just £7.00, delivered direct to my door. Post and packing is free, and there's a free Newsletter. If I choose not to subscribe I shall write to you within 10 days - I can keep the books and gifts whatever I decide. I can cancel or suspend my subscription at any time. I am over 18.

Mrs/Miss/Ms/Mr _____   EP94M

Address _____

_____

_____ Postcode _____

Signature _____